Meet Hate

Winter Falls ~ Dempsey Sisters #4

D.E. Haggerty

At Arm's Length
Hands Off
Knee Deep
Molly's Misadventures

Chapter 1

🦋

I GLIMPSE THE SIGN for Winter Falls as I approach the small town and slow down to read it. The population has been crossed off and replaced with a smiley face smoking a joint. All right then. This town might be my kind of place after all.

My sisters – or, rather, two of my sisters – have been bragging to me about this small town in Colorado since they discovered it a year ago. Until Mr. Smiley showed up, the thirty-minute drive from civilization hadn't impressed me much. But now? Things are looking up.

Sirens blare behind me and I swear underneath my breath. So much for things looking up. My foot automatically presses on the acceleration to speed up. *Stop it.* I am not *that* woman anymore. I will not run away from the consequences of my actions any longer.

Liar.

I ignore the voice in my head. I'm trying to be better. I am.

I slow down and pull off to the side of the road. The police car stops behind me. The sirens switch off but not the lights.

Is this small town police officer trying to intimidate me? How cute.

The car door opens and I watch as the cop steps out. Judging by how long those legs are, he's a tall one. Awesome. I do love a tall man since I'm five-eight. All of us Dempsey girls are tall. Except Gabrielle. She's a midget.

The cop saunters toward my car, his long legs eating up the distance in no time. Confidence looks good on this man. As does his lush, brown hair. Hair perfect for threading through my fingers as his mouth devours mine. At the thought, tingles erupt throughout my middle.

Phew. My libido is back. I was worried my desire to have sex would never return. I've never been so happy to be proven wrong in my life. And I hate being wrong.

He arrives at the car and scowls at me while motioning for me to lower the window. Oops. I guess not all of my rebel tendencies have been squashed. What can I say? I'm a work in progress.

I hit the button to lower the window and flash him a flirty smile.

"Hi, Officer. Was I doing something wrong?"

Feigning innocence is step one of the 'How Olivia Handles Police' manual. I consider batting my eyelashes, but small town police don't need the full 'Olivia Effect',

"License and registration," he grumbles.

My hands tighten on the steering wheel. Has he never heard of the word please before? I clench my teeth before any sarcasm can spill out. I'm a law-abiding citizen now. I don't mouth off to the police. I inhale a cleansing breath before making certain my smile is firmly affixed to my face.

"Of course, Officer."

I dig the registration out of the glove compartment. As I hand it to him, I bat my eyelashes – guess he's getting the full 'Olivia Effect' after all – and repeat my earlier question. "Was I doing something wrong?"

My innocent display isn't entirely an act. I'm pretty certain I wasn't committing a crime. Unless gawking at the town sign counts as a crime. Don't worry. It doesn't. I know the law books as well as, if not better than, the police.

I shove those thoughts away. That's *Past Olivia* speaking. I've mostly tamed her, but she enjoys sticking her nose in my business from time to time.

The officer flips his sunglasses on top of his head and smiles at me. I swallow my gasp. His sexy long legs and lush hair have nothing on his handsome face.

His eyes are the color of dark chocolate and when he smiles a dimple pops out on each side of his face. I want to stick my tongue in those dips and taste his skin. Best of all? He's clean shaven. I know beards are all the rage, but I enjoy scraping my fingernails over a man's jaw while I kiss him senseless.

I lose his eyes when his gaze dips to check the registration. "Beckett Dempsey. You don't look like a Beckett."

"He's my brother."

He scowls. "Beckett is your brother?"

"Do you know Beckett?"

"Answer the question."

There's no sign of those adorable dimples now.

"Yes, Beckett is my brother. I'm his sister."

He holds out his hand. I reach forward to shake his but he grunts, "License," before our hands can meet.

I feel my cheeks warm but I've never let a little embarrassment stop me before. *New and Improved Olivia* will not be embarrassed by a slight misunderstanding. I remove my license from my wallet and offer it to him.

His nose wrinkles as he studies the Missouri license. I think I hear him mutter *stupid out of towners* but I'm not about to ask him to clarify. I know when to keep my big mouth shut.

"Olivia Lucy Dempsey."

"That's my name. Don't wear it out."

He glowers at me. Someone lost his sense of humor. Considering those dimples, I'd ask him if he needs my help locating it, but the police uniform has me holding my tongue. There's a time to flirt with a police officer, but this isn't it.

"From Missouri."

I widen my eyes to stop myself from rolling them. I also manage to somehow keep the duh I want to speak from slipping out. Go *New and Improved Olivia!*

"Yes, I recently relocated to Colorado."

"You'll need to get a Colorado license if you're staying."

I'll add 'brave DMV hell' to my never-ending to-do list.

"How come I've never heard of you before?"

"Because I'm not famous," I quip. Notorious maybe. But famous? Nope. Not interested either. You can't get away with shit when the paparazzi follow you around everywhere.

He rolls his eyes. "I know you're not famous."

Gee. Way to make a girl feel special.

"But if you're Beckett's sister, why don't I know your name?"

"I assure you I am Beckett's sister. Trust me. I know who my brother is."

This is quickly becoming the most confusing conversation I've ever had with a police officer. And I've had some interesting conversations with law enforcement before. They ask the strangest questions. Such as 'Why are you wearing a bikini in a snow storm?' As if the answer isn't obvious.

"I've never heard you mentioned before."

Ouch! Why don't you go ahead and shoot me in the chest with your gun? The pain wouldn't be nearly as bad as being reminded of all the problems I'm having with my family. Like I don't already know.

I ignore the pain – I should be used to it by now – and dial up the innocent level on my smile.

"I'm sorry, Officer. I don't know what to tell you except Beckett is definitely my brother and Gabrielle, Elizabeth, and Cassandra are most certainly my sisters."

He studies me for a moment before offering me my license and registration.

"Aren't you going to write me a ticket?" The question pops out of my mouth before I can stop it.

"Since Beckett's your brother, I'm sure you know the rules."

What in the world is he blathering about?

"The rules?"

He frowns. "About driving a gasoline engine in Winter Falls."

My nose wrinkles. "Gasoline engine?"

He sighs. "You do know a car has an engine?"

I open my mouth to snark at him, but I snap it shut before the words rush out. I clear my throat. I am *New and Improved Olivia*. I no longer rant at police officers. Even when they deserve it.

"I'm aware, but I don't understand why we're discussing driving a gasoline engine in town."

"I guess *your family* didn't tell you about Winter Falls after all."

The way he says family makes me think he doesn't believe I'm Beckett's sister. Why would I claim to be the sister of a man if I'm not? Does he think I'm some sort of con artist? I wish. But I'm not a good enough actor to pull off a con. Plus, my mouth often has a mind of its own.

"They didn't mention gasoline engines."

Huh. My comment comes out snark free. Maybe I could be a con artist after all. Too bad *New and Improved Olivia* promised to walk on the right side of the law.

He motions to the front of the car. "This car has a gasoline engine." He cocks an eyebrow at me and I nod. "Gasoline engines are forbidden in Winter Falls."

My eyes widen. "As in no one in town has a car?"

I can't believe neither Gabrielle nor Elizabeth mentioned this in all their raving about the town. Then again, we don't exactly engage in long gabbing sessions. Our conversations usually involve a whole lot of me claiming to be fine before hanging up.

"Most people drive golf carts or use bikes."

"But how do they get to town?"

"Tourists," he spits the word out, "are allowed to drive to the Inn on Main. There's a public parking area there."

"Okay. Thank you for the information, Officer."

He nods before putting on his sunglasses and strutting back to his car. I wish I could say I didn't watch him walk away, but I'd be lying. This man's ass is epic and worth all the ogling in the world. I'd love to squeeze it, but it's pretty obvious he's not a fan of mine. He didn't even bother telling me his name. Rude.

I frown as I switch the engine on and drive away. I don't understand why my sisters are gaga about this town. Although, if all the men are as good-looking as the grumpy police officer, I can understand the appeal. I'll put up with a buttload of grump for a sexy man.

Police officers are off limits, *Past Olivia* reminds me. As if I need the reminder.

Chapter 2

Peace – a man who has absolutely no interest in being matched by a bunch of interfering old ladies

✦

PEACE

"Good afternoon, Peace," Sage greets as I enter the police station.

"Afternoon," I respond and keep on moving.

I know better than to stop. Sage is the police dispatcher, but her true calling is gossiping. She even refers to herself and her friends – the other town busybodies – as the gossip gals.

Unlike her gang, I have no interest in knowing everyone's business. Let people have their secrets. As long they aren't hiding criminal endeavors, I don't need to know.

"Meet anyone interesting today?"

I pause. Her question does not bode well for me. In addition to being the biggest gossip in Winter Falls, Sage fancies herself a matchmaker. Thus far, I've mostly managed to avoid her scheming. I hope my luck hasn't run out.

"I've been out patrolling."

"You didn't stop anyone interesting?"

At her question, I glance back at her in time to catch her fluttering her eyelashes in innocence. Innocent my ass. The woman is up to something, but I refuse to fall for it. She can't possibly know I pulled Olivia Dempsey over. My pulse races as I recall my first glimpse of Olivia.

The woman is a wet dream. Blonde curly hair I want to fist in my hand. Plump, pink lips I'd love to see swollen from my kisses. Alabaster skin that has me wondering what color her cheeks turn when she blushes. Not to mention how far the blush will travel down her body.

And then there's her attitude, which shouldn't intrigue me but does anyway. Her cheeky smile makes me think she's hiding a secret. Considering her blue eyes sparkle with mischief, she's probably hiding more than one secret.

I catch Sage studying me. Shit. She can't know what I'm thinking about Olivia. The gossip gals are relentless with their matchmaking.

And I refuse to be involved in one of their schemes. The last time they interfered in my dating life, things didn't turn out the way I expected. They used me. I won't be used again.

"Nope," I say and hurry down the hall to the main area of the station where my desk is.

My colleague and fellow police officer, Freedom, bursts into laughter when I enter the room. "You're up next!"

"I am not up next."

"You totally are." He rubs his hands together in excitement.

I glare at him. He thinks because he's gay, he's safe from the matchmaking schemes of the gossip gals. I wouldn't put it past those women to find him a match. They'll import one if they have to.

Although, there's a man in Winter Falls who he has his eye on. He thinks I don't know. Did he forget what I do for a living?

"This is a place of work," I remind him because, unlike the rest of the townspeople, I take my job seriously.

Someone giggles before the chief's door opens and his wife tumbles out. Her messed up hair and wrinkled shirt make it clear what they've been up to. I roll my eyes as Lyric, the chief of police, struts out behind his wife.

"Dude, she's ready to pop your baby and you can't keep her hands off of her?" Freedom teases.

"It's my fault," Lyric's wife, Aspen, claims. "Pregnancy hormones make you horny."

Lyric snickers behind her. "I'm merely doing my duty to my wife."

I chuckle. "I think you mean doing your wife."

Sage rushes into the room. "Any backache? Extra urge to use the bathroom? Do you need to poop?"

Aspen rolls her eyes. "I'm not going to discuss my bowel movements with you."

"I don't know why not. I changed your diapers as a baby."

This is Sage's excuse for being nosy, although I've yet to figure out what the connection between changing someone's diaper and invading their privacy is.

"Whatever," Aspen mutters. "I'm not in labor. The baby's not due for several weeks."

I eye her belly. She looks ready to go into labor any minute, but my wager doesn't have her delivering the baby for another four weeks. She better not go into labor prematurely. I'm determined to win a bet for once.

"Sex can't bring on labor, can it?"

Aspen points at me. "You better not have bet on when my baby's born."

Of course, I placed a bet on when the baby's birth will happen. Everyone in town has. Betting is the town hobby. But I don't mention this to Aspen. You never know how a pregnant woman is going to react.

I raise my hands and smile making sure my dimples pop out.

She wags her finger at me. "You can't use your dimples against me."

My smile deepens and she covers her face with her hands.

"Help! He's wielding his dimples."

Lyric growls before spinning her around and grasping her wrists to pull her hands away from her face. "I've got dimples."

"Yeah, but your dimples can't be shown in public."

"Why not?" Sage asks. "Public nudity isn't a crime in Winter Falls."

She's not joking. Except for weekends when there are festivals and the town is flooded with tourists, public nudity is allowed. Sometimes, it's encouraged. Like when we go skinny dipping in the river near the falls the town is named for, for instance.

"Stop ogling my husband, Sage!"

"But it's one of the benefits of my job. It's in the contract."

Lyric sighs. "The contract you wrote and signed without my approval?"

"Would I do such a thing?"

"Bane of my existence," he mutters before tugging Aspen toward the exit. "I'm done for the day."

"I hope not." She giggles and he quickens his stride.

I wait until Sage has followed the couple out of the station before asking Freedom, "Do you know how many sisters Beckett has?"

I don't need to explain who Beckett is. The advantage of a small town is how everyone knows everyone. Of course, the disadvantage of a small town is how everyone knows everyone.

He scratches his chin. "Let me see. There's Gabrielle, Cassandra, and Elizabeth."

"What about a fourth sister?"

He shrugs. "I'm not sure." He studies me. "Why?"

"No reason."

I don't tell him about pulling Olivia over. When I first set eyes on her, I thought I hit the jackpot. But then she claimed to be Beckett's sister. A sister no one has heard of. Since there are no secrets in Winter Falls, I'm not buying her story. I could hardly claim she was a liar without proof, though.

I switch on my computer. Time to find some answers.

"Why are you asking?"

I avoid his gaze and concentrate on typing my password. "No reason."

His chair squeaks as he stands. "No reason? This is going to be fun. Any chance you want to give me the inside scoop so I can win the bet? I'll split my winnings with you."

"There will be no bet."

He pats my shoulder as he passes me. "You're cute. Sage probably has the odds already calculated."

Sage doesn't know everything, I remind myself. She can't possibly know about my attraction to Olivia. It doesn't matter anyway. Being attracted to a stranger is meaningless. Especially if she isn't who she says she is.

I glance at the clock on the wall. "Don't you have somewhere to be?"

My question is rhetorical. I know he has somewhere to be. He goes to White Bridge every Thursday night. I don't know where he goes or what he does, and I don't care. He's entitled to his privacy even if everyone else in Winter Falls doesn't realize the word privacy exists.

He snorts. "This conversation isn't over."

I wait until the door shuts behind him before I open up the program to do a background search on Olivia Dempsey.

I'll be damned. She is Beckett's sister. I wonder why no one talks about her.

I notice she has a criminal file and open it. As I read about her various arrests, I realize why no one has mentioned Olivia before. She's not merely the black sheep of the family. She's a bad seed.

Not in my town. I won't let her ruin Winter Falls with her criminal tendencies.

Chapter 3

✦

"THANKS FOR MEETING ME," I tell my sisters, Elizabeth and Gabrielle, as I join them at a table in the bar I chose in the town of White Bridge. "I had to get out of the house before I punched Beckett in the face. I swear if he asks me one more time what I'm doing with my life …"

I shouldn't complain about Beckett. My brother did offer me a place to live while I get my life together – again.

Gabrielle nods. "I know what you mean."

Elizabeth grunts. "Mr. Overprotective strikes again."

Overprotective is putting it mildly. When our parents died in a car crash, I was fifteen. Beckett took over raising us despite being a teenager himself.

Being our guardian switched a flip in him. Before, he was a fun older brother who teased us constantly. When he became responsible for us, he transformed into this overbearing and super protective man I barely recognized.

"I can't believe you're living with him and Lilac."

I sigh at Elizabeth's comment. I don't want to tell her I have nowhere else to go. It's the truth, but I don't need her pity. I'll be back on my feet soon enough.

"I love Lilac. She's perfect for him," Gabrielle says.

I shrug. "She's not the type of woman I expected him to end up with."

Don't get me wrong. Lilac is nice and all, but she takes everything literally. I told her I need to figure out my next steps and she asked if I wanted a referral to a podiatrist. It literally took me three minutes to realize she wasn't joking.

"I can't wait until they start having children." Elizabeth looks all dreamy at the idea. She would. She's always wanted a big family.

"I'm surprised you haven't gotten knocked up yet."

Elizabeth is currently living with River, her best friend she fell in love with. He's also the older brother of Phoenix, Gabrielle's fiancé. Who ever thought my sisters would end up falling in love with brothers?

"I promised Lilac I wouldn't get pregnant before her wedding."

I chuckle. Lilac is the only woman in the world who could get Elizabeth to make such a promise. Generals preparing to attack the enemy are jealous of how my future sister-in-law is planning her wedding. Everything is organized down to the most insignificant detail.

A waiter arrives and plunks a pitcher of beer and three glasses down on the table. Elizabeth reaches for the pitcher and her elbow knocks over the glasses. Gabrielle doesn't bat an eye as she catches them before they roll on the floor.

"Personally, I prefer to drink from a glass and not the pitcher," I tease Elizabeth.

"I swear those glasses weren't there two seconds ago."

"Really?" I lean close to whisper. "Was it magical? Maybe we're in the Flunky Cauldron?"

Gabrielle clears her throat. "It's the Leaky Cauldron," she corrects in a soft voice.

I know exactly what the name of the pub in the Harry Potter world is. Who do you think read all seven of those books to my baby sister at bedtime every night? But it's my duty as the oldest sister to tease her as much as possible.

Elizabeth slides a beer across the table to me and another to Gabrielle. "The two of you will have to drink this pitcher. I'm driving." She meets my gaze. "Since you didn't want to meet up in Winter Falls."

There was no chance of us meeting in Winter Falls. There's exactly one bar in the small town – *Electric Vibes* – and my sister Cassandra manages it.

Gabrielle squeezes my hand. "Her bark is bigger than her bite."

Easy for her to say. She's not the one who pissed Cassandra off. Cassandra is fun – if a bit crazy – but when you get her mad, watch out. She can hold a grudge like no one's business

I'm not saying she doesn't have the right to be mad at me. She does. I screwed up, but I'm taking responsibility for the consequences of my actions. Albeit a bit late for Cassandra's liking.

But I have no intention of discussing my issues with Cassandra today. Time to change the topic of discussion.

"How's Phoenix?" I ask Gabrielle.

Her cheeks darken and she ducks her chin. "Good."

I wiggle my eyebrows. "Good? Not great? Does he not rock your world?"

Her face flames and she lifts her glass and guzzles half the beer. I raise mine and salute her before downing the contents.

Elizabeth snorts. "He totally rocks her world. When he's not playing with his goats."

"Isn't he a goat farmer?"

From what I understand, Gabrielle's fiancé is a biological goat farmer outside of Winter Falls. Everything in Winter Falls is biological or ecological or whatever the proper term is for products developed in a carbon neutral town founded by a bunch of hippies.

I don't pretend to understand what any of it means. I should probably take one of River's green tours to learn more, but I've got enough going on in my life at the moment.

"There's nothing wrong with a goat farmer," Gabrielle says.

"I never said there was."

"Don't worry about her," Elizabeth says as she refills my glass. "She's a bit sensitive about the goat thing since Cassandra is convinced her goats are little devils."

I was wondering how long it would be before they brought up Cassandra again. I sip on my beer as I contemplate how to answer without falling into the Cassandra trap.

"Why would a goat be the devil?"

Elizabeth waves away my question. "Cassandra's just scared of the goats."

So much for avoiding the Cassandra topic. I sip on my beer as I formulate my response.

"There's nothing scary about goats," I claim, despite never having been in close proximity to one before.

"I agree, but every time Cassandra is near a goat she ends up on her knees."

"On her knees?" I choke out.

"You know. Begging the—"

My bark of laughter cuts off whatever she was going to say. Elizabeth has the habit of accidentally blurting out sexual innuendos. Her cheeks darken until her face is the color of a ripe tomato. As a redhead, it's impossible for her to hide her blushes. Which, of course, means I try to get her to blush as often as I can.

"What about you, Olivia? Is there a special man in your life?" Gabrielle asks.

At the reminder of the last 'special' man in my life, I snatch my beer. I was such a fool. I finish the drink in one gulp. Elizabeth's eyebrows lift, but she doesn't speak as she pours me another glass.

I reach for the glass and the room spins. I clutch the table and wait for my balance to return. What the hell? I haven't had more than a few beers. I shouldn't be feeling any effects. Olivia Lucy Dempsey can hold her alcohol.

Although, I haven't been drinking much for the past few months. Turns out *New and Improved Olivia* is a bit of a tee-totaler. I never would have expected that.

Elizabeth studies me. "I think Olivia has a special man."

I roll my eyes. Oops! Not a good idea when your balance is precarious. I wait a few seconds until my vision clears.

"I'd rather discuss Cassandra than my relationships."

What the hell? Where did those words come from? I stare at the glass in my hands. Alcohol always gives me loose lips syndrome. I narrow my eyes on Elizabeth. Is she deliberately trying to get me drunk so I spill my secrets?

"Don't worry. I'll drive you home," she says as she fills my glass again.

"Are you trying to get me drunk?"

She winks. "There is no try."

I switch my glare to Gabrielle. "And you agreed to this plan?"

Her cheeks darken but she holds my gaze. "I did."

"Why?"

She clears her throat. "Because I don't want anyone in the family fighting. You and Cassandra used to be thick as thieves."

Elizabeth elbows her. "Do you remember the time the police brought them home from the strip club? They'd auditioned to be dancers. Olivia was convinced she was Alex from that old movie *Flashdance*."

"Hey! No dissing *Flashdance*. It's one of the best movies ever made."

Elizabeth giggles. "Beckett was livid when he found out you performed the scene from the movie where she dumps water all over herself for your audition. You were sixteen and supposed to be in chemistry class."

"Chemistry is such a waste. I have not one day in my entire life used a single thing I learned in chemistry class."

Elizabeth grunts. "Probably because you didn't learn any-thing. What was the name of the guy who did all her homework for her?"

Gabrielle taps her chin. "Davis Doolittle."

"Davis Doolittle? He didn't speak to animals or have adventures on an island with a crew of strange pets." Although, it would have made him much more interesting if he did.

Elizabeth snaps her fingers. "David Doyle! That was his name."

"I fail to understand why we're discussing ancient history."

I pick up my glass but the beer sloshes over the side. Maybe I've had enough to drink. Whoa. Where did that voice come from? I have never in my life slowed down once I've begun to drink. *New and Improved Olivia* waves her hand. *It was me.*

"Not speaking to your sister for the past two years is hardly ancient history."

Damn it. I couldn't have a family that's afraid of confronting issues. That pretends everything's fine even when things are definitely not fine. I blame Beckett. He's the one who always made us discuss our problems when we were teenagers.

"I just want her to forgive me, you know?"

Crap. Loose lips syndrome strikes again!

"What happened?" Gabrielle asks and I have to bite my tongue before I snarl at her. My anger must be clear to see in my eyes, though, since she raises her hands in surrender. "I'm just trying to understand. Cassandra's the one who always stuck up for you with Beckett. Who bailed you out of jail when you needed it. She covered for you all the time. What happened?"

I bite my tongue before I admit what an idiot I was.

"Does it matter? What's the point in rehashing the past?"

Elizabeth throws her head back and roars a laugh. I throw a peanut at her. She bats it away as she wipes tears from her eyes.

"Have you met Cassandra? She's not going to forgive you until you fess up to your mistake. All of your mistakes."

Which is what I'm afraid of. How do I tell my sister how stupid I've been?

Chapter 4

Six-pack — an excuse to strip off your clothes

❧

PEACE

I scowl as Sage and her posse rush toward me.

Freedom laughs next to me. "Told you, you were next."

I growl. I will not be the next target of one of the gossip gals' matchmaking schemes. I won't allow it.

I pound his shoulder, which only makes him laugh harder.

"I can't be next," I claim. "There's no one to match me with."

Despite my words, my mind conjures up a picture of Olivia. My body tightens at the vision. It's ridiculous. The woman is a criminal. And I'm a police officer. I would never date a criminal.

"No one to match you with?" He snorts. "You're funny."

"And you're shit out of luck the next time you need someone to cover a shift for you on Thursday night."

"It's cute how you think you can resist my charm."

The gossip gal gang stops in front of us. In addition to Sage, the group includes Feather, Petal, Cayenne, and Clove. Together the five of them are a force of nature best avoided. Especially if you're single and not looking to be paired off with someone of their choosing.

Petal fans herself as she glances between the two of us. "Maybe we should match Peace and Freedom. They are adorable together."

Feather nods in agreement. "They remind me of the couple in *Red, White & Royal Blue*."

Cayenne taps her chin as she studies us. "Who's the prince and who's the president's son?"

I've had enough. I try to leave but Freedom throws his arm around my shoulders to stop me. "Can I be the prince?"

I shove him away. "Knock it off. You should know better than to encourage them."

Sage pats Freedom's chest. "You've always been such a good boy."

"Are you fondling him?" Clove asks.

Sage's hands roam over Freedom's chest. "I think I feel a six-pack."

Clove elbows Sage out of the way. "Let me feel. My Sirius has never had a six-pack."

"Shall I remove my shirt for you ladies?" Freedom winks. "You can snap pictures if you want."

Petal removes a camera from her oversized bag. "Strip!"

The rest of the women chant with her. "Strip! Strip! Strip!"

While everyone concentrates on Freedom who is indeed now removing his top and strutting around pretending he's in a fashion show, I sneak off. I'm going to give him so much shit when the gossip gals decide to match him.

My eyes roam the area as I make my way through the crowd. I'm on duty today but there's no sense patrolling as everyone in town will be at this party. The party is to celebrate Cedar and Cassandra moving in together. Although, Cedar still needs to ask Cassandra to move in with him. They're currently 'chatting' in the wooded area behind the house while everyone gathers in the front yard.

Cedar grew up in Winter Falls but then he took off wandering after high school and has only recently returned. He decided to stay when he fell in love with Cassandra. Olivia is Cassandra's sister, but Cassie never mentioned her before. Probably because Olivia is a troublemaker who doesn't belong in Winter Falls.

Speaking of troublemakers. I frown when I catch sight of Olivia. I intercept her before she reaches the bar.

"What the hell are you doing here?"

She sneers at me before her expression changes and she feigns confusion. "What am I doing here? Cassandra is my sister. What are you doing here?"

Is she seriously trying to act innocent? I know damn well she doesn't have a clue what the word means. I grasp her arm and drag her away from the crowd.

She yanks her arm from my grip. "You have no excuse to manhandle me. I'm not committing a crime."

Not currently she isn't. Give it time, though, and she will.

I bend close and hiss at her. "I looked into you."

She claps and my nostrils flare at her utter disregard for my authority. "Good job. You're a police officer and you know how to perform a background check. Your mamma must be very proud."

"Your sarcasm is duly noted."

"Are you going to write down how sarcastic I am in your little notebook?" She widens her eyes. "I'm scared."

I'm about done with her whole innocent act. I may be a police officer in a small town, but I'm still a police officer and she doesn't fool me for one second.

"You're going to ruin your sisters' lives."

She flinches. Huh. Am I wrong about her? Does she actually care about anyone besides herself?

"It's none of your business."

Nope. She doesn't care about anyone else. She's selfish and self-centered. It's hard to believe she's related to the rest of the Dempsey sisters. Gabrielle's sweet as pie, Cassandra's hard working, and Elizabeth is—

I force thoughts of Elizabeth out of my mind. Now is not the time to think about what happened there.

"It's my business when you bring your troubles to town."

She opens her arms wide. "What troubles? I've brought nothing to town."

Does she think she's fooling me? I wasn't born yesterday.

"You don't need to bring anything. You're trouble all by yourself."

Before Olivia has a chance to answer, Elizabeth rushes across the yard. "Olivia! I didn't realize you were here."

Elizabeth wraps her arm around Olivia. "Do you need help?" she whispers, but I hear her. She doesn't wait for Olivia to reply before stepping in front of her to shield her. "Peace, good to see you."

A flare of pain flashes through me. For a moment, I thought Elizabeth could be the one. I knew she had her heart set on River, but I never thought he'd give up his playboy ways for her. I was wrong. I'm happy for her, but I can't help thinking of what might have been.

"Hi, Elizabeth."

"Have you met my sister, Olivia?"

River chuckles as he saunters our way. "Obviously, they've met, Bessie."

Elizabeth threads her arm through Olivia's. "Shall we get a drink and go spy on Cassandra and Cedar?"

"Sounds good."

Olivia waves to me as she wanders away with Elizabeth. I scowl at her.

"Who are you scowling at?"

I startle at Lyric's question. I didn't hear my boss coming up behind me. Freaking Olivia. She totally made me forget I'm supposed to be working.

"Olivia Dempsey."

"There's a fourth Dempsey sister?"

"Yep. And there's a reason no one discusses her."

He scratches his beard. "I trust you'll keep an eye on her. Make sure she doesn't get into trouble."

This isn't the Chief of Police speaking. The Chief doesn't ask me to keep an eye on residents. No, Lyric has obviously been ensnared in Sage's matchmaking plans.

"You have got to be kidding me. You've teamed up with the gossip gals?"

"You can't blame me. Babies are expensive."

"And you think you can win the bet."

He winks. "We can win together."

"Let me make things clear. I want nothing to do with Olivia."

Would I enjoy tying her to my bed and having my wicked way with her? No. I wouldn't. Because she's a criminal. The twitch in my cock makes me a liar.

He crosses his arms over his chest and frowns down at me. At six-foot-three, he's one inch taller than me and he never lets me forget it.

"She's not a criminal."

"You're wrong. Of course, she is. I ran her record."

"And was she convicted of any of those charges?"

"Have you been snooping on my computer?"

Lyric isn't the type of boss to keep a tight leash on his employees. He's laidback. As long as we perform the tasks we've been assigned, he doesn't bother us with how we perform them.

"Answering a question with a question. Sage would say you're being evasive."

I snort. "You're quoting Sage now? The woman who you refer to as the bane of your existence."

"Lyric!" Aspen waddles our way holding her stomach. "I'm hungry."

"She's always hungry," he mutters before flashing her a smile. "Then, we shall get you some food to eat."

The tension leaves my body when he leaves, but he doesn't make it far before glancing over his shoulder at me. "Think about what I said."

What he said? He's out of his mind. Olivia is a criminal.

You aren't charged with as many crimes as she has been unless you're up to no good. It doesn't matter whether she was convicted of any charges or not. Her family has money. They probably paid someone off to get her out of trouble whenever she landed in it.

The gossip gals have lost their minds trying to match me – a police officer – with a criminal. They're in for a surprise because

I am not going to follow along with whatever scheme they've cooked up. I am my own man with my own mind.

Chapter 5

Disclaimer – Pickle Penis Shots do not include any parts of the male anatomy

✦

I step out of Lilac's car at *Electric Vibes* and stare at the bar my sister, Cassandra, owns and scowl. I do not want to be here. But I was given no choice.

Today is Lilac's bachelorette party, and the bride-to-be told me, in no uncertain terms, I was expected to attend or else. She didn't leave the 'or else' hanging either. Nope. If I didn't come, I was supposed to sit at home and write an essay about my future plans. I don't know if the woman is always this pushy, but as an upcoming bride, she has the market cornered on pushy.

I spot my brother, Beckett, strolling across the parking lot. "What are you doing here?"

Lilac wags her finger at him. "Oh no, you don't. You are not going to have your bachelor party the same night as my bachelorette party."

He drags her into his arms before planting his lips on hers. I look away. I do not have any desire to witness my brother making out with his fiancée. And, yes, I realize how ironic I'm being considering I waved my sexual adventures in his face at every opportunity when I was a teenager.

While I'm waiting for the two lovebirds to finish playing kissy face, Gabrielle and Elizabeth arrive on bikes. They lean their bikes against the wall of the bar before waving to me.

"Aren't you going to lock those up?" I ask.

Elizabeth giggles. "This is Winter Falls."

"Saying the name of the town isn't an answer to a question."

"Yeah, it is."

I focus on Gabrielle. Maybe she doesn't speak in riddles. But she shrugs and repeats, "It's Winter Falls."

"Is there something in the water here? Or have you both been smoking the wacky weed?"

"Now. Now. Nothing wrong with wacky weed," an older man doing an impressive imitation of a hippy says as he wanders past us.

"Who was he?"

"Lennon," Elizabeth answers as she tugs me toward the entrance of the bar. "He thinks he's the reincarnation of John Lennon."

"Didn't John Lennon die in 1979?"

I quickly calculate. There's no way this Lennon guy could be the reincarnation of the Beatle. The dates don't work. And I'm not convinced reincarnation isn't a bunch of hogwash.

Then again, what do I know? I thought— I mentally slap myself upside the head. I am not going there.

Someone mutters, "I hate math." And I turn around to find an extremely pregnant woman waddling toward us.

"I'd explain how math is for losers but. Must. Pee. Now," the pregnant woman says as she pushes her way past us and rushes off.

"That was my sister, Aspen," Lilac introduces as she joins us with Beckett following her.

"What is Beckett doing here?" Elizabeth asks.

"That's what I said!" I shout and we high-five each other.

"He's not staying." Beckett grunts and Lilac glares at him. "He may have one beer and then he's leaving."

"K-pow!" A woman feigns cracking a whip. "Someone's whipped."

Lilac sighs. "This is another sister of mine, Ashlyn."

"I'm her favorite sister," Ashlyn claims.

"Please." Another woman snorts as she joins the group. "You're no one's favorite."

Ashlyn wiggles her eyebrows. "I'm pretty sure I'm Rowan's favorite."

"Whatever." The woman rolls her eyes. "I'm Ellery. The second oldest West daughter."

"West daughter?"

"There's five of us in total." She points to Lilac. "She's a West." She points to the door Aspen ran through. "She's a West." She points to Ashlyn. "She's a West."

Ashlyn wags her finger. "Nuh-uh. I am no longer a West." She offers me her hand. "You must be Olivia. Dempsey sister number four."

I shake her hand and she uses her hold on my hand to draw me near. "Rumor has it you're a crazy troublemaker, which is my kind of gal." She leans forward to whisper, "But if you hurt

Cassandra, I will glitter bomb you so bad you'll be peeing glitter in your eighties. You got me?"

Peeing glitter? I start to smile but wipe the humor from my expression when she snaps her teeth at me. "Yes. I got you."

"Awesome! We're going to be the best of friends."

"Hey!" A woman shoves her way in between us. "I'm supposed to be your best friend."

Ashlyn throws her arm around the intruder. "And you are. Totally."

Together they skip into the bar. More crazy people. They seem to congregate in Winter Falls. I do love a bit of crazy in my life. I'm beginning to understand the appeal of this small Colorado town.

"Who was she?"

"Moon, Ashlyn's best friend," Ellery answers.

My brain is about to overload, but I do know how to count. "You said five West sisters. I'm counting four – Aspen, Ashlyn, Lilac, and Ellery."

A car pulls up and stops in front of us. I know next to nothing about cars, but an idiot can tell this vehicle is worth some serious dough. I expect some glamorous person to step out, but a woman in jeans and scuffed boots slides out of the car.

"Thanks for the ride." She blows the driver kisses before slamming the door.

"This is the last West daughter – Juniper," Lilac explains.

"Hi!" Juniper waves in greeting.

I indicate her hair. "I think you have straw in your hair."

She giggles as she shakes her hair out. "Yep. Straw. Good catch."

"She didn't have a roll in the hay. She manages the wildlife refuge outside of town," Elizabeth explains.

Juniper winks. "I can have a roll in the hay *and* manage the refuge."

"Shall we go inside?" Lilac taps her watch. "My party should have started three minutes ago."

Juniper whips out a salute. "Yes, Captain Timekeeper. Whatever you say, Major Boring."

"How do I have two names?"

"I don't know, Lilac Bean West. How do you have two names?"

Lilac's nose wrinkles. "Why am I getting the middle name treatment?"

Juniper ignores her and marches for the door. She holds it open while motioning for us to go inside. "After you, Bride To Be."

I wait until everyone's inside before creeping to the door.

"What's wrong?" Juniper asks. "Don't you enjoy partying?"

"She enjoys partying!" Elizabeth responds from inside the bar. "But she's afraid of our sister."

Juniper threads her arm through mine and drags me inside. "This is interesting. Why are you afraid of your sister? Wait. Which sister?"

I nod toward the bar where Cassandra is standing with her arms crossed over her chest shooting daggers out of her eyes at me.

"Oh boy. She is one pissed off bartender. I hope she doesn't put laxatives in our drinks."

I better not tell her about the time Cassandra added cherry-flavored milk of magnesia to our cherry vodka sours. It was a shit show. Literally.

"Maybe I should leave."

Juniper's hold on my arm tightens. "Ha! If you think you're leaving and depriving me of my day's entertainment, you are sadly mistaken."

"The roll in the hay wasn't satisfying?" I tease.

She barks out a laugh. "I'll make sure to tell Maverick what you said."

"She's referring to Maverick Langston," Elizabeth explains.

My mouth gapes open. "Maverick Langston, the movie star?"

Juniper blows a raspberry. "Nope. In Winter Falls, he is simply Maverick, the fiancé of Juniper the Magnificent."

Ashlyn elbows her. "Since when are you the Magnificent?"

"Nice of you to join us for this *family* activity," Cassandra says as she approaches.

Crap on a cracker. Is she doing this now? Is she going to air all her grievances against me at this very minute? In front of everyone? I glance around the room and notice everyone is watching us.

A group of gray-haired women wearing hot pink t-shirts with the words *I Was Told There'd Be Strippers* on them wave at me while giving me the thumbs-up signal. I guess the crazy in this town is not limited to the younger generation.

Before I can ask who the women are, Elizabeth arrives and shoves a champagne glass in Cassie's hand. "Here. Drink this. It's cotton candy champagne. It'll calm you down."

"I know what it is. I mixed these drinks." She sets the drink back down on the tray. "I better not drink. I need to have my complete faculties for when it's time to bail Olivia out of jail."

I flinch at Cassie's words. I won't deny she's bailed me out of jail before, but I'm not the person who used to get a kick out of being arrested anymore. I'm trying to be better. She obviously has no faith in me. Although, she hasn't seen me for two years and doesn't know about my grand plans to become the *New and Improved Olivia.*

"Does Olivia get arrested often?" Lilac asks.

"I'm not going—"

Cassie cuts me off before I can defend myself. "Often enough."

"I'm Lilac's designated driver. I won't be drinking at all tonight."

Ashlyn holds up a tray of pickles. "Not even a penis pickle shot?"

I can't help a giggle from escaping. "Penis pickle?"

Cassie swipes the tray from Ashlyn. "These are not supposed to be served until later. Where did you get them? Never mind." She narrows her eyes at me. "It's pickle juice and tequila. None for you."

I ignore the pain slicing through my chest and raise my hands in surrender. "I won't be drinking."

"Olivia and tequila is not a combination Winter Falls can handle."

Ashlyn leans close. "Do tell."

I've had enough. I need a break from Cassie's negativity. I'll get a breath of fresh air outside, reinforce my shields, and come back.

I stride toward the exit, but before I can reach the door, it bangs open and Peace rushes in.

Shit on a shingle.

Chapter 6

❧

PEACE

A cheer goes up as I enter *Electric Vibes.* "Who-hoo! The stripper has arrived."

One guess who's cheering. I glance over at the gossip gals. I sigh when I read what their t-shirts say. *I Was Told There'd Be Strippers.*

I stalk to the bar. Cassandra grins at me, and I can't help but notice how beautiful she is. Her blonde hair and fair skin remind me of Olivia. I growl. I don't want to think about Olivia and beauty in one sentence. Criminal. Remember?

"I was contacted about a disturbance."

Cassie's eyes widen and she glances around the room. "I don't know anything about a disturbance."

I run a hand through my hair. I was afraid of this. "The call came from your landline."

I'm not a complete idiot. Everyone knows Lilac's bachelorette party is today. There are bound to be shenanigans.

Ashlyn rushes to my side and holds up a shot glass. "Blowjob?"

I cock an eyebrow and stare her down. "Where's Rowan?"

She glares at me. "Rowan is not the boss of me!" She stomps her foot and the liquid in the glass spills out over her hand. "Oops! I guess I have to drink it now."

She downs the shot and licks her lips. "Yummy!"

I groan. Rowan is going to kill me when he finds out about this. Ashlyn's husband is not what you refer to as 'laid back'. The former NFL quarterback is protective of his wife. I don't know why. Ashlyn can take care of herself.

I notice her pirouetting in front of me. "Since when does Ashlyn know ballet?" I ask the room.

"She doesn't." Cassandra motions toward Ashlyn who's now spinning around with her arms thrown wide.

She hits a table and bounces away only to trip on air. Before she can fall, I reach forward and grab her elbow.

"Thanks, Peace." She pats my chest. "Ha! You're a police officer and your name is Peace. Did you know another name for police officer is officer of the peace?"

She giggles at her own joke until she's snorting and gasping for air. Cassie hands me a glass a water. "I think someone had one too many pickle penis shots."

"Pickle penis shots? I don't want to know."

I hand Ashlyn the glass and she downs it in one go before slamming it on the bar. "Barkeep, another!"

"I don't think she knows it's water," Cassie murmurs as she refills the glass and hands it to her.

"Enough of this chit chat. Time for a dance!"

Feather herds me away from the bar and into the middle of the dance floor.

"You hired a stripper?" Olivia asks.

Olivia's here? I search the room for her. She's standing beside Lilac with a notepad in her hand. What the hell is she taking notes about?

"I'm not a stripper. I'm a police officer for the town of Winter Falls. I'm not allowed to earn any additional money other than my salary."

"Actually," Lilac begins and I spear her with a glare. She's undeterred. "The rule you quoted applies solely to the chief of police. It does not apply to the police department in general."

I rub a hand down my face. "I'm not here to strip." My eyes meet with Olivia's. "I'm here because someone called in a disturbance."

Hurt flashes in her eyes before she blinks and it's gone. Maybe I imagined it?

She raises her hands in the air. "I didn't do it, Officer."

Sage points at Olivia. "It was her! She did it."

Olivia's eyes widen. "What are you going on about? I didn't do anything. Who are you?"

Sage pushes Olivia in my direction. "I'm your fairy god-mother." Olivia plants her feet.

"Help me!" Sage hollers.

"I'll help!" Ashlyn yells and runs toward them straight into a table and tumbles to the floor.

Cassandra sighs as she helps Ashlyn to her feet. "Since when is Ashlyn the clumsy one? Isn't it Elizabeth's job to be a klutz?"

"Hey!" Elizabeth stomps her foot. "I'm not always a klutz."

Olivia snorts. "Yeah, you are." She turns to Gabrielle. "Do you remember the time she fell at the school assembly while she was going up the stairs to the podium and showed everyone her panties?"

Gabrielle giggles. "And Beckett hadn't done the laundry, so she was wearing the cookie monster ones?"

Elizabeth's face darkens. "Must you remind everyone of every single embarrassing moment in my life?"

Cassie wraps an arm around her neck before rubbing her knuckles over her hair. "It's our duty as your big sisters."

"Exactly!" Olivia agrees and Cassie frowns at her.

Olivia tucks her chin into her chest but not before I glimpse the pain in her expression. I want to wrap my arms around her and take away her pain. I mentally berate myself. *No, I do not.* Olivia is a criminal and not for me.

Suddenly, music blares from the speakers. I sigh when I recognize the song – *Blurred Lines.*

"I'm not stripping!" I announce to the entire bar.

"But you can," Sage says. "There's nothing stopping you."

I cross my arms over my chest.

Clove claps and squeals, "Whoa! Check out those biceps!"

I drop my arms. "I'm on duty, ladies."

I snort. Ladies? The gossip gals are many things, but ladies is not one of them. Genteel? Not hardly.

Feather and Cayenne herd Olivia forward toward me. "What are you doing? I can't dance. I'm supposed to be taking notes, so Lilac knows what gift was from whom."

"Don't worry, Olivia. I have a photographic memory."

At Lilac's announcement, Oliva whirls around. "Seriously? You can remember everything you see?"

"Yes, a photographic memory refers to the ability to remember—"

Juniper slams a hand over Lilac's mouth. "It's your bachelorette party. You shouldn't be quoting definitions."

Lilac pulls Juniper's hand away. "She asked. It's rude to not answer a person's question."

While the two argue, the gossip gals manage to wrangle Olivia until she's standing on the dance floor with me.

"What's going on? Who are these women?"

"These are the matchmakers of Winter Falls."

"The best matchmakers in Colorado," Feather corrects.

"I thought we agreed to say we're the best matchmakers this side of the Mississippi?" Sage forms the words into a sentence, but she's not asking. She's the leader of the group and as such, she's firmly of the opinion that what she says goes.

"I don't understand how any of what you've said has anything to do with me." Olivia's nose scrunches in confusion. It's adorable. No, it's not. I've obviously been working too much if I think a criminal's nose is cute.

Ashlyn slides to a halt next to me. "I know!"

"What happened to your shoes?"

"Shush now." She squishes my lips together. "The adult type people are making words now."

I remove her hands from my lips. "How much have you had to drink?"

She raises a finger. "Two pickle penises." She giggles. "It's a tongue twister. How many times can you say pickle penises? Pickle penises. Pickle penises. I like penises."

I groan. "Shall I phone Rowan to pick you up?"

"Rowan! I like his penis best of all!"

"Rowan's her boyfriend, isn't he?" Olivia asks.

"Boyfriend! Rowan isn't my boyfriend! He's my husband. And I love him. And his penis. I love his penis, too."

Rowan enters the bar and marches to us. Good. He can handle his wife.

"Dream girl." Rowan wraps an arm around her waist to pull Ashlyn near.

"He means me. I'm his dream girl. He's my dream penis."

Rowan chuckles before throwing Ashlyn over his shoulder. "We're out."

"Bye!" Ashlyn waves. "I'm leaving to go play with Rowan's penis."

Once they leave, Olivia clears her throat. "Well, I'll be getting back to…" She trails off as she motions toward the group of women who are standing around Lilac. All of whom are watching us.

"You can't leave," Sage hollers. "You're his match."

"And he's yours," Petal adds.

I glare at them. "I'm not going to be the target of one of your matchmaking schemes."

"Tsk. Tsk." Clove wags her fingers. "You didn't have a problem participating in our matchmaking schemes when Elizabeth was involved."

It takes longer for Olivia to wipe the pain from her expression this time. Fuck.

Elizabeth rushes up to us and grasps Olivia's hands. "It was only one date. Don't be upset on my account."

Olivia jerks her hand free and scratches her neck. "I'm not upset on your account."

"She's lying," Cassandra claims. "She's scratching her neck. It's her tell."

Olivia growls. "Great. Make sure the cop knows my tell."

I step closer to her. "Sounds as if someone brought trouble into town after all."

Her nostril flares as she stares me down. "I did not bring trouble into town."

Elizabeth wiggles her way in between us. "Hey now. There's no reason to argue."

I rub a hand down my face. "Sorry, Elizabeth."

Olivia fists her hands at her side. "To her, you apologize? I've done nothing to you and all you do is accuse me of being a criminal."

"I've seen your record."

She reaches around Elizabeth to poke me in the shoulder. "Which has zero convictions!"

"You don't get arrested multiple times unless you're guilty of something."

She throws her arms in the air. "I'm done." She stomps away.

"Go ahead, Olivia. Run away. It's what you do best," Cassandra hollers after her. Olivia stumbles but not for long.

She slams out of the bar and Elizabeth turns on Cassandra. "She's trying, Cassie. Maybe you could lay off and give her a chance. Being hard on her is not helping anyone."

"Maybe if she'd learn how to apologize," Cassandra grumbles under her breath.

"If there's no disturbance." I hurry out of the bar before any of the gossip gals can waylay me.

I'm in time to hear a car door shut when I get outside. Olivia better not be driving when she's angry. I march toward the car but halt when I notice she's not in the driver's seat. She's sitting in the back. At least this one time she made the right choice.

She better be careful, though. Because I'm ready and waiting for the time she doesn't make the right choice.

Chapter 7

Pivot – when you change your game plan, because the current one has gone to hell

❧

I MAKE SURE TO drive several miles under the speed limit as I enter Winter Falls. The last thing I need is for Peace to pull me over. The guy hates me. No. Hate isn't a strong enough word. He loathes me. He loves Elizabeth, though. My grip tightens on the steering wheel.

I'm not jealous of my sister. I'm not! But I don't understand what I did to Peace to make him hate me. Yes, I've been arrested once. Okay, more than once. But I've never been convicted of a crime. Whatever happened to innocent until proven guilty?

I inhale a few cleansing breaths as I park in front of *Earth's Bliss*. I have more important things to worry about than Peace, the not very peaceful man.

Earth's Bliss is a yoga studio. I can't believe a town the size of Winter Falls has a yoga studio. On the other hand, the town was founded by hippies so maybe I shouldn't be surprised.

Since I'm a certified yoga instructor, I contacted the owner to ask if she had any job openings. She messaged me yesterday to ask me to meet with her today. Squealing may have been involved when I read her message.

I've never interviewed for a job with someone who I don't already know. This is a huge leap for me. I close my eyes and mumble the mantra for the *New and Improved Olivia*.

I am present in this moment. I am conquering my fears.

I repeat the mantra until I feel my heartrate slow to a normal pace and my muscles release their tension. Once I'm calm, I open my eyes. I'm ready.

I scan Main Street as I walk from my car to the yoga studio. I have to admit this town is adorable. It's quaint and cute. It could be the set of a Hallmark movie. Except there's a man walking his squirrels down the street. He waves at me and I rush inside *Earth Bliss.*

Me and squirrels are not friends. I swear you hide out from police in a tree one time and the entire species never lets you forget about the squirrel that toppled to the ground during your escape. I took the poor animal to the emergency vet, but I've yet to be forgiven.

"Welcome!" A woman greets upon my entrance.

My brow wrinkles. She's one of the elderly women who were trying to force me and Peace together at Lilac's bachelorette party. Damnit. This is a set up. I shouldn't have gotten my hopes up.

She hurries forward and grasps my hands. "Don't leave. Please. I've been waiting for your arrival."

I check my watch. "I'm on time."

She giggles as she leads me further into the building to a small office where she deposits me on a chair.

"Don't be silly. I've been waiting for your arrival in Winter Falls."

I'm confused. Colorado wasn't exactly a planned relocation for me.

"What do you mean?"

"You are the person I've been waiting for."

Thanks for clearing things up. Things are about clear as mud now.

"You've been waiting for me? Did my sisters tell you I was coming?"

Impossible. No one except Lilac knew I was moving to Colorado. I haven't exactly been good about keeping in touch while I living in Saint Louis. Thus, the whole rift with Cassandra.

"No. No. No." She waves her hands in front of her. "I'm not explaining this well."

I keep my mouth firmly shut as she sits in the chair behind the desk. I'm not about to tell my hopefully new boss she's not good at explanations.

"Let's start over. I'm Cayenne. Nice to meet you."

"Hi, Cayenne. I'm Olivia," I say although she obviously already knows my name.

"I've been waiting for a young person such as yourself to arrive and assume control of the business. I knew if I put my wish out there into the universe, the universe would answer."

Assume control of the business? What is she talking about?

"I thought you asked me here to discuss my teaching a few classes."

"I didn't want to scare you away."

I blow out a breath as I repeat the words, *I am conquering my fears* in my head.

"I think there's been a misunderstanding. I can't take over your business." Here comes the difficult part. "I don't have the funds." And no bank would give me a loan. Who can blame them?

Her nose wrinkles. "You don't? Aren't you a Dempsey?"

And here's the reason I didn't want to follow my brother and sisters to Colorado. I don't want to be a Dempsey girl. Hold up. I mean I do want to be a Dempsey. I'm proud to be a Dempsey. But I don't want everyone making assumptions about me because I am a Dempsey. Assumptions such as me having tons of money because the family is wealthy.

"I am a Dempsey."

"Well, then. There's no problem."

I am conquering my fears.

"I don't have any money." My family has money. I don't. Big difference.

She frowns. "Oh dear. I'm afraid I assumed." She waves her hands in front of her face. "Never mind what I assumed."

I force a smile. "I could still teach a few classes, though, if you need an extra instructor."

She plants her elbows on the table and places her chin in her hands as she studies me. I need all of my training not to squirm under her perusal.

"Nope."

I prepare to leave. "Thank—"

"I still want you to take over the studio."

I freeze at her proclamation. "But I don't have the money."

"I'm going to finance you."

I must have misheard her. "You're going to finance me? But you don't know me. I'm a notorious bad bet."

Past Olivia snarls. *What are you doing? Free money!* She throws her arms in the air and squeals *Whee!*

She smirks. "I do love an underdog."

"But…" My voice trails off when the door bangs open and three women rush in.

Cayenne bounces to her feet to greet them. "Olivia. This is Feather, Clove, and Petal."

These women are from Lilac's bachelorette party, too. I search the area for an exit.

"Please stay," Cayenne pleads.

Clove steps closer. "Don't worry, dear, we're not here to matchmake you."

I frown. "You seemed awful keen to matchmake me before."

And it's not embarrassing to be matched with someone who hates your guts. Not at all.

Petal dismisses my words with a wave of the hand. "That was all Sage."

There's another one? I don't bother disguising my desire to escape now. I inch toward the door.

"She's not here. She's working," Feather explains.

I test the waters. "And you don't want to matchmake me with Peace?"

Cayenne snorts. "Of course not. You two are obviously not a match."

Despite her being correct, I flinch at her words. Peace is one sexy cop. In another life, I would have jumped at the opportunity to spend some time between the sheets with him. And promptly used his position as a police officer to win me favor. *Past Olivia* doesn't exactly understand what morals are.

Hey! Past Olivia shouts. *I know what morals are. I choose to ignore them is all.*

I pretend not to hear her. She doesn't rule my life anymore. Besides, Peace isn't interested in me. He's made his feelings about me abundantly clear. Elizabeth, on the other hand, he—

"A police officer and a troublemaker?" Feather giggles. "It would never work out in the end."

I appreciate her use of the word troublemaker instead of criminal. Peace loves to say I'm a criminal. I'm not. I've tangled in misdeeds is all. It's not the same thing.

But there's one thing I'm not clear on. "If you're not here to match me, what are you doing here? Is there a yoga class now?"

Clove lifts up a cup of coffee. "We're here to meet the latest business owner in Winter Falls as we're all business owners ourselves."

"You are?" I clear my throat when I realize how skeptical I sound. "Sorry. I shouldn't assume. What businesses do you own?"

Cayenne points to Petal. "She owns *Sensual Scents.* She makes organic candles. Feather owns *Feather's Frozen Delights*. It's the ice cream shop next door."

"My products are homemade and organic," Feather explains.

"And I own the coffee shop, *Clove's Coffee Corner,* next door." Clove hands me the cup of coffee. "Here go you."

I sniff the coffee, but it isn't coffee, it's tea. "How did you know?"

She winks. "It's my superpower. I know a tea drinker when I come across her."

She would have been wrong a year ago. A year ago, I couldn't drink enough coffee. Or smoke enough cigarettes. Or drink— I shut down those thoughts. I won't let the past rule me.

I take a sip. Honey lemon green tea. Yummy. "Thank you." I smile at the rest of the women. "And thank you for the welcome."

I didn't dare hope the people of Winter Falls would welcome an outsider such as myself. I've never lived in a small town before, but I assumed they wouldn't embrace strangers. Peace's response was more what I expected.

"Of course. Of course. We look forward to getting to know you better." Feather's words are pleasant, but I don't trust the gleam in her eye.

"Shall I contact you about an appointment to discuss the business?" I ask Cayenne as I inch toward the door.

"We need to get through next Wednesday night first."

I freeze. Her response makes no sense. "Wednesday night?"

"It's the monthly business meeting." My gaze must telegraph my confusion because she explains, "All new business owners need permission from the town before beginning their endeavors."

"I need permission from the town?"

This was a waste of time. They're never going to grant me permission to manage *Earth Bliss.* Cayenne might be willing to support an underdog, but the rest of the town will see me for what I am – a failure.

Clove pats my arm. "Don't worry, dear. We have your back. 'Have your back' is what the young people say isn't it?"

"Um. Yes."

She claps. "Wonderful. See you Wednesday."

I wave and hurry away before I find out more bad news. Once I've driven out of Winter Falls, I pull to the side of the road to get my breathing under control.

I place my hands over my chest and wait for my heartrate to calm down. I feel as if I just got off of a rollercoaster ride. But, unfortunately, this rollercoaster ride didn't end with an exhilarating loop. Nope.

This ride will end on Wednesday when the town makes it abundantly clear what they think of Olivia Dempsey, the loser, acquiring a business in town.

This will teach me to never get my hopes up again.

Chapter 8

Guilt trip – completely legal means to blackmail someone into doing what you want them to

You have to come.

I scowl. I'm not a fan of being told what to do. The words 'have to' and 'must' are banned from my vocabulary. You'd think Elizabeth had figured that out by now.

Plus, she's referring to the opening of the community center in Winter Falls. The same community center Cedar Hansley, aka Cassandra's live-in boyfriend, is in charge of. It's the last place I want to be today.

Please come.

Dang it. Gabrielle knows I can't resist her begging. My baby sister has been using this knowledge against me since the second she realized she had me wrapped around her little finger.

Fine.

Leave the grumpy at home.

Elizabeth got her way. She doesn't need to push it.

We'll meet you there.

Good grief. How many people are invested in me attending the opening of the community center? I don't bother responding to Beckett's message. He already knows I'm attending because apparently, my sisters can't keep their mouths shut.

Except for Cassandra. She hasn't responded to any of my messages. I don't dare phone her. Being hung up on by your sister isn't exactly a boost to self-confidence. But I forced myself to send her a message after the fiasco at the bachelorette party. Her response? Complete and utter silence.

Proving what a complete fool I am, I tried again. This time the message wasn't even read.

Since the Winter Falls community center is next to *The Inn on Main* where there's a large parking lot for tourists, I decide to park there and walk to the opening.

Past the inn is *Bohemian Treasures.* I stop to window shop at the jewelry store. It's not your typical jewelry store with all kinds of bling. Instead, the items here appear to be handmade. And, okay fine, I may be procrastinating.

I force myself to continue to the community center. The doors stand wide open, but I hesitate at the entrance.

"Yeah! You're here." Elizabeth drags me inside by the arm. "I thought we agreed you'd leave the grumpy at home."

River wraps an arm around her waist and pulls her away from me. "She's here. Let her be."

I flash a smile of thanks at him. I could use an ally while I redeem myself with the family. And his application for the position was just accepted.

Maa.

A goat bumps into my leg while bleating its little heart out. "What's a goat doing inside?"

"Not you, too." Gabrielle sighs but she doesn't explain what she means. "And Pan's wearing a diaper, so she's allowed inside."

Phoenix chuckles as he strolls over to us. "Gabrielle refused to leave her at home."

Gabrielle bats her eyelashes up at him. "Pan was crying. She didn't want to be alone."

He tweaks her nose. "Because she's got you wrapped around her little finger."

"I think you mean paw," I say.

Elizabeth laughs. "Good one."

"What are you laughing about?" Cassandra asks as she joins us. When Elizabeth shuffles to the side, allowing Cassie to notice me, she scowls. "Never mind."

Before she can escape, Elizabeth grasps her hand. "We were making fun of Pan."

Cassandra jumps back. "The goat's here? Inside?"

Gabrielle pats Pan's head. "Don't take it personally, Pan. She has a prejudice against goats."

"I'm not prejudiced against goats. There's no such thing. But I do have a problem with farm animals being inside. Especially when inside is the community center my boyfriend is officially opening today."

Gabrielle motions toward the goat. "She's wearing a diaper."

"Who's wearing a diaper?" Cedar asks before he kisses Cassandra on the cheek and draws her near. My sister practically melts into him.

I creep backwards. Cedar was none too happy to meet me the one time I saw him at Beckett's house for a family dinner. Needless to say, there hasn't been another family dinner since then.

My mantra pops into my mind. *I am conquering my fears.* And my feet halt. Conquering my fears? Yes. Let's do this.

"Hi, Cedar. Congratulations on the opening."

Cedar's gaze slides to Cassandra before he responds. "Thank you."

"Are you planning to have any type of exercise classes for the kids who frequent the center?"

He clears his throat. He's obviously uncomfortable with the conversation, but I will not give up. Conquering my fears.

"Yes, my brother, Rowan, already offered to teach some."

"Great!" *Be brave, Olivia.* "What about yoga classes? Do you have any interest in those?"

"I hadn't thought about yoga."

"Yoga is great for children. It can help them manage their anxiety, improve their self-esteem, increase body awareness, and develop strength and flexibility. There are all kinds of benefits."

I may be gushing. What can I say? Discovering yoga saved my life. Literally.

"Even if all of those benefits are correct, what does this have to do with you?" Cassandra asks. She's not scowling, though, so I consider this a win.

"I'm a yoga teacher."

Her eyebrows fly off of her forehead. "You? You're a yoga teacher?"

Elizabeth steps in. "You shouldn't be surprised. She's super flexible. Remember the time we were out to eat and Beckett claimed she couldn't put her leg behind her ear."

"I remember Beckett screaming and claiming he was going to take her to the emergency room."

"Me?" Beckett shoves his way into our circle. "I never scream."

Lilac grunts beside him. "You're lying."

"I'm lying for dramatic purposes. It's not considering lying then."

Her nose wrinkles. "Is this a rule? No one told me about this rule."

"It's not a rule," I tell her. "He's yanking your chain. And he totally screamed when I put my leg behind my ear. Here, let me show you…"

"Stop!" Beckett slaps at my hands. "Please don't."

"Why does this freak you out?" Lilac asks. "You enjoy my flexibility during coitus."

Big brother's face darkens to a shade of red I've never seen on him before. Awesome. Maybe Lilac being super literal isn't a bad personality trait after all.

"Do not mention us having sex in front of my sisters," he grits out between clenched teeth.

"Why not? They know we have sex." She motions to my sisters with a sweep of her arm. "And they have sex, too." She frowns at me. "Except Olivia. I don't know what her sex life currently entails."

Cassandra rubs a hand over her forehead. "I never thought I'd say this before, but can we please return to the topic of why Olivia is a yoga teacher?"

"You're a yoga teacher?" Beckett asks. I nod. "When did this happen?"

"Why did this happen is the more interesting question," Cassandra mutters but I pretend I don't hear her.

"I've been working on my certification for the past year."

I don't want to discuss why I choose yoga as a profession. My reasons are a conversation for when we're alone. Not when we're surrounded by a whole town of people. The population of this town may be limited to one-thousand people, but that's about nine-hundred-ninety-nine people more than I want to discuss my private life with.

I clear my throat and address Cedar. "Anyway, I wanted to offer my services. For free, of course! But I could teach a yoga course to the kids once a week."

"Phone me and we'll set up an appointment to discuss things," he offers.

"I will," I promise as we shake hands.

Cassandra's staring at me as if I'm an alien from Mars she's never seen before. "You can't make commitments if you're not going to stick around."

"Who said I'm not going to stick around?"

I moved all my crap to Colorado, didn't I? I gave up my apartment. Said good-bye to my friends. Friends. Another conversation for another day.

"You're not exactly the most reliable person in the world."

Since she's not wrong, I don't lash out at her. "I'm trying."

Elizabeth nudges Cassandra. "You should give her a chance."

Cassandra gazes up at Cedar who shakes his head as he backs away. "Don't ask me to get in between you and your sisters."

Cassie scowls. "You're supposed to be on my side."

"Princess, I am always on your side." He kisses her hair. "But you know how I feel about family."

She rolls her eyes. "Way to guilt trip me."

He smirks. "Did it work?"

"No."

My shoulders slump in defeat. Gaining Cassandra's forgiveness is harder than I thought it would be. I already thought it'd be harder than learning how to do a one-handed tree pose. And it took me six months to learn that pose.

"Fine," Cassandra grumbles. "I'll give Olivia a chance." She glares at me. "But one chance is all you get. Blow it and we are done for good."

"Hey now," Beckett says before I can respond. "People make mistakes."

"Does anyone remember the time Cassandra pushed Cedar away because she was a big, fat scaredy-cat?" Elizabeth asks and everyone in the group except me raises their hands.

Before I have the chance to ask what the hell they're talking about, Cassie stomps her foot. "Fine. You get two chances. But I expect an explanation and an apology."

An explanation? Gulp. An apology I can do. I'm not certain if I can explain, though.

"Don't worry," Gabrielle whispers. "Cassie's explanations didn't make any sense either."

I have no idea what Gabrielle's talking about, but I smile at her in thanks for her encouragement.

"Deal."

Cassandra and I bump fists before someone calls for Cedar's presence to begin the presentation and they leave.

As I watch my sister walk off without a backward glance, I consider my explanation. I'm screwed. How the hell am I going to explain without appearing the fool?

Chapter 9

❧

FOR SOMEONE WHO DOESN'T live in Winter Falls, I sure spend a lot of time here. Although, I'll probably move to town if the community approves my acquisition of *Earth Bliss*. Then again, I'm not sure Winter Falls is big enough for both Cassandra and me.

But I'm proud to announce there have been improvements in the 'Olivia will get Cassie to forgive her'-movement. I messaged Cassie some stupid meme about goats and she sent back a LOL emoji. Baby steps!

Today's trip to Winter Falls is for the monthly business meeting. The meeting in which the town votes on their approval of me as a business owner. Gulp.

I asked Cayenne what I should prepare – a business plan, a cash flow prognosis, etc. – but she told me to come as I am. And then she started humming a Nirvana song. Before she could begin her imitation of Kurt Cobane, I agreed and hung up.

And now I'm arriving for this business meeting woefully unprepared. Shit. Maybe Peace is right. I should tuck my tail and flee before I ruin my sisters' lives.

I am conquering my fears.

Damn mantra. There's obviously a reason I choose it. I knew becoming the *New and Improved Oliva* would mean overcoming my fears. I didn't realize my fears needed to be conquered every freaking day.

Knock! Knock!

Elizabeth raps on my car window. "Are you going to stare at the building all day or are you coming inside?"

I open the car door.

"Good choice," she says as she winds her arm through mine. "They have beer and popcorn."

I skid to a halt. "What? Beer and popcorn? Isn't this the monthly business meeting?"

"There's no reason for it to be boring."

I'm beginning to understand why every answer to every question about the town is answered with 'It's Winter Falls'. This place is a world unto itself. We continue on our way to the courthouse where the meetings occur.

A woman passes us muttering, "Let's get this shit show over."

"Who is she?"

"Eden. She's the current mayor."

"She doesn't sound happy to be mayor. Why'd she run for the position if she didn't want it?"

"There's not an election for mayor," River explains from behind us.

I glance back at him to discover there's a crowd making their way inside the courthouse. "Does everyone come to these meetings?"

"Gabrielle and Phoenix don't." Elizabeth leans close as if she's going to tell me a secret. "Phoenix is a bit of a loner. He doesn't enjoy coming to town."

"Your baby sister is good for my brother. Forces him to leave his goats once in a while," River adds.

I snort. "Except he brought a goat to the community center opening."

"Goat!" Ashlyn peeks her head out of the building entrance. "Where's a goat?"

"Dream girl," Rowan sighs.

"What? I like goats. Everyone likes goats."

"I hate goats," Cassandra mutters as she marches up the steps.

"Where's Cedar?" Elizabeth asks.

"At home, playing loner."

"Come on." Ashlyn nabs my hand and drags me into the meeting room. "The line for beer and popcorn is atrocious."

Rowan grunts. "As if I'd ever let you stand in line." He kisses her hair before marching off to stand in line.

Ashlyn winks at me. "Works every time."

She doesn't give me a chance to reply before she's manhandling me toward the front row where the rest of her sisters are waiting. She shoves me into a chair and sits next to me. Juniper is on my other side.

"Welcome to crazy town," Juniper greets.

Rowan returns and hands Ashlyn a pitcher of beer and a few glasses.

"Who's not pregnant or nursing?" Ashlyn asks as she hands out the glasses.

"I'm driving," I remind her when she tries to hand me a glass.

"Are you sure?" She waggles her eyebrows.

"Um, yeah." How does she think I arrived here? On my broom? I keep those thoughts to myself as Cassandra already thinks I'm a witch. No reason to add fuel to the fire.

Lilac clears her throat. "Um, Olivia. Feel free to drink if you want. I'll drive us home."

"Don't you have your own car?"

Her lips purse. "Beckett dropped me off before rushing off to a client meeting. This is the last time we share a ride. I've told him numerous times how—"

"So, you can drink!" Ashlyn interrupts and shoves a glass toward me. I grab it from her before it ends up in pieces on the floor. "Today's word is 'but'."

"Word of the day? What?" Winter Falls is beyond confusing at times.

"Every time someone says the word of the day, you have to drink," Juniper explains.

"And she decided a conjunction was the best word of the day? Is she trying to get us drunk?"

She shrugs. "It's Ashlyn."

I'm pretty sure her answer means yes.

"Are you ready for this?"

I freeze with the glass at my lips. "Ready for what? Cayenne said I didn't need to prepare. Damnit. Should I have prepared?"

Cassandra bursts into laughter. "This is going to be fun."

I don't get a chance to answer before the mayor claps her hands to gain everyone's attention. Lilac stands and joins her at the front of the room.

"What is Lilac doing?"

"She's the town magician," Ashlyn answers.

"She means she's the town comptroller," Juniper explains.

"Do you get an allowance for being Ashlyn's interpreter?" I ask and she chuckles.

"The first order of business is the transfer of the business *Earth Bliss* to Olivia Dempsey. All those in favor?"

"Hold on!" I jump to my feet. "But aren't you going to vet me first?"

"Drink!" Ashlyn taps my glass.

"Are you crazy? I'm discussing my business with the mayor," I hiss at her.

"This is Winter Falls," is her response. Proving she is, indeed, crazy.

"I agree with Olivia," someone hollers and I squint toward the back to discover Sage waving her hand. "Olivia is an outsider. Maybe someone from the committee should discuss her goals, etc. with her before we vote as a town."

"The committee? What committee?"

"Usually, a committee vets the businesses on Main Street." Ashlyn hiccups.

"Then, why was the matter brought to a vote?"

Maybe I should drink more beer and then all of this will make sense.

"I assumed no one would have a problem with Olivia since her family is tied to the town," Cayenne answers.

"Wrong!" Crap. I know that voice. "I object."

Of course, Peace objects. The man objects to anything having to do with me.

"This is getting good," Juniper mutters and I glare down at her.

"Don't blame me. I'm bored. Maverick is away shooting another film."

Ashlyn leans forward in her chair to answer Juniper and nearly ends up scrawled on the floor. "You're blaming your boyfriend for being bored? Lame."

I reach forward to help Ashlyn, but Elizabeth shoos me away. "I got her."

I confront Peace. "Can I ask what the nature of your objection is?"

He crosses his arms over his chest and I can't help but notice how his biceps strain against his t-shirt. Can't help? Yes, I can. I am not ogling his body. No way. I force myself to meet his gaze.

"I think you know what my objection is."

I raise my eyebrows. "I do?"

"Do you want me to spill all of your secrets in front of the whole town?"

Sage raises her hand. "I want you to spill all of her secrets."

The rest of her friends nod in agreement. I glare at Cayenne and she shrugs.

I address Lilac and Eden. "How shall we proceed?"

Lilac opens her mouth, but she doesn't get a chance to answer before Petal does.

"This sounds like a personal matter between Olivia and Peace. I vote they meet privately to discuss if they can put aside their differences for the sake of *Earth Bliss.*"

I narrow my eyes on her. Petal and her friends promised they wouldn't try to matchmake me with Peace anymore.

She bats her eyelashes. "I'm not matchmaking. I'm seeking a solution to this problem."

I don't believe her, but Eden is already putting the matter to a vote.

"All in favor of Olivia and Peace proceeding with the matter privately say aye."

A round of ayes go up, including from all the people I'm sitting with.

"The matter is settled. Olivia, set up an appointment to meet with Peace."

"But I didn't get a chance to object."

Lilac nods. "Despite the overwhelming majority of the group agreeing with the matter being settled privately, it is important to follow procedural rules."

Eden grunts. "All opposed say nay."

I practically scream 'nay'.

"Duly noted and ignored."

I stand. "I'm out of here."

"But you didn't finish your beer." Ashlyn points to the glass I'm holding. "And I said but. Twice! Drink. Drink."

I down the rest of the glass and hand it to Juniper before marching straight out of the meeting.

This is ridiculous. I can't believe the town is forcing me to meet privately with Peace because he's being a dickwad. He doesn't care about my ability to manage a business. He wants me out of town because he hates me.

I'm seriously starting to think I harmed him in a previous life. Maybe reincarnation is real after all.

Chapter 10

Yoga outfit – the downfall of many a righteous man

◆

PEACE

The smell of incense hits me as I enter *Earth Bliss.* I study the business Cayenne has built. In front of me is a reception desk with a small waiting room. Off to the side is an office. The main attraction – the large studio area – is straight ahead.

The rear wall is all windows allowing light to flood into the area. The soft color of the maple hardwood floor helps to maintain the light and airy feeling as does the mirror covering one wall of the room. The wall opposite the mirrored one is dotted with shelves of plants.

"You're here. You're early," Olivia greets as she exits her office.

I whirl around to confront her, but the words die in my mouth when I catch a glimpse of what she's wearing. If this is how women dress for yoga, I need to consider attending some classes.

She's wearing a sports bra on top showcasing her toned abs and lean arms. On the bottom, she's wearing a pair of leggings that accentuate her curves. Curves my fingers long to touch.

I run a hand through my hair. Olivia is not the woman for me. I shouldn't be fantasizing of all the ways I can make her scream while she's naked. I scowl.

"Oh. Sorry." A blush spreads from her cheeks down her neck to the top of her breasts.

I bite back a groan. She is not helping the situation in any way.

"I'll um …" She rushes off to the office and returns with a sweater. She puts it on, but it's cropped and doesn't hide those toned stomach muscles.

"Freaking gossip gals," I mutter.

"Gossip gals?"

"It's how *we* refer to Feather, Petal, Sage, Cayenne, and Clove." I can't help emphasizing we. She's the outsider here. Not me.

She frowns. "Isn't labeling someone a gossip rude?"

I snort. Olivia the criminal is worried about hurting someone's feelings? I don't believe it. "They love the name. They even have t-shirts with the name printed on them."

A smile lights up her face. "Awesome."

I growl. "You're enjoying how they're trying to match us?"

Her nose wrinkles. It's adorable. *No, Peace, it's not adorable.* Nothing about this woman is adorable.

"They're not supposed to be matching us anymore. I spoke with Cayenne and the rest of them. They said they wouldn't try to match us anymore."

I cock a brow. "And you believed them?"

"Of course! Why wouldn't I? They're a bunch of sweet old ladies."

I bark out a laugh. "They have you totally fooled."

She motions to the studio around us. "Cayenne offered to help me finance the purchase of her business. Her offer is the very definition of sweet in my book."

"Cayenne is helping you finance the purchase?" She nods. "But you're a Dempsey."

She glances away as she scratches her neck. "I… um… don't want to use the family money."

She's lying. Even if I didn't know her tell is scratching her neck, I'd know she's lying.

"You're lying."

Her head whips up and her eyes narrow at me. "How dare you call me a liar."

I cross my arms over my chest and plant my feet on the floor. "You're not denying you lied."

All the bluster leaves her. "I don't have any money."

"You don't have any money? The Dempseys are rich. And you're a Dempsey."

She sighs. "Should we sit down?"

She doesn't wait for my response before collapsing on a chair in the reception area. I follow suit and sit across from her.

"Maybe if you can't afford the studio, you shouldn't buy it."

Her eyes flash with hurt. "It would make you happy if I didn't buy the studio, wouldn't it?"

I don't respond since confirming how I would indeed enjoy her leaving town makes me a complete asshole. I'm not an asshole. I'm merely looking out for the good of my town. Known criminals living in town is not good.

"What does it matter to you? Cayenne wants to retire. Isn't it better if the business continues instead of shutting down? No one wants an empty storefront on Main Street."

"Cayenne wants to retire?" This is news to me.

"She wants to travel. Go on a quest or whatever she called it."

I frown. Cayenne leave town? She's an integral part of this place. I can't imagine her not being here every day.

Olivia grins. "Maybe you don't know everything happening in town after all."

I lean back and cross my arms over my chest. Her eyes dip to my biceps and I can't help but flex them. She bites her bottom lip. I should be the one biting her plump, pink lip. I clear my throat. I need to stop these thoughts about Olivia. She's a criminal, I remind myself.

"Enough about the town. We need to discuss why you acquiring this studio is not going to work."

"Not going to work? You're not even going to give me a chance?"

"Why should I? You don't have the money to buy the studio, you're an out-of-towner, and you have a criminal record."

She rears back. "You hate me," she whispers.

"I don't hate you." Hating people is not allowed in Winter Falls. I'm not kidding. The town was founded by hippies. Hippies are all about love and peace. Hate is not allowed.

"You do. I've never done anything to you and yet you hate me for who I am."

I flinch at her words. She makes me sound prejudiced. I'm not prejudiced. I didn't judge Olivia before I met her. I'm judging her based on what I know. She's a criminal.

"I've paid for my crimes. Don't I deserve a second chance?"

Paid for her crimes? She hasn't done any jail time. How the hell has she paid for her crimes?

"There's more than one way to pay for a crime."

"Disagree. There's only one way to pay for a crime. Via our criminal justice system."

She snorts. "Do you seriously not know how broken our justice system is?"

I grit my teeth. Is she making fun of my profession? I've dedicated my life to justice and she thinks it's a joke.

"Our justice system isn't broken."

She rolls her eyes. "Really? And there's not a bunch of men on death row in Texas who are innocent either."

I open my mouth to argue with her but slam it shut again when I realize we're off topic here. Way off topic. I swallow my anger and state, "We're not here to discuss the criminal justice system."

"No. We're here to find out why you hate me."

Hell. This topic is not any better than the criminal justice system.

"I don't hate you, but we are going in circles here. I don't think we can come to a resolution."

She jumps to her feet. "Come to a resolution? You haven't even tried to resolve anything. You waltzed in here with your preconceived notions of me and made zero effort to discuss the situation. You haven't asked me one word about my business plan, my cash flow analysis, my—"

I stand. "I'm not—"

She wags her finger at me. "Yes, you are. You're not listening to me. You're merely—"

I do the one thing guaranteed to get her to stop yelling. I slam my lips down on hers. As soon as her wild taste hits me, I moan. This is a mistake.

Her hands grasp my t-shirt and pull me near until I can feel her breasts straining against my chest. Her nipples harden and I forget why this is a mistake. Why I'm questioning this.

Screw it. If I'm making a mistake, I might as well enjoy it. I bite her lower lip and she gasps allowing me to shove my tongue into her mouth. Her fingers tighten on my t-shirt as I devour her mouth.

But she isn't some innocent bystander. There's nothing innocent about this woman. Her tongue flirts with mine until I growl and palm her neck to draw her even closer.

My phone buzzes in my pocket. I yank my mouth from Olivia's. Crap. What have I done?

Her hazy eyes glance up at me and she smiles.

"We shouldn't have done this."

Her smile falls from her face, and she steps away from me. "Save me from your 'this was a mistake speech'."

She doesn't bother to wait for my reply before marching off to her office. My gaze follows her perky ass displayed to perfection in those tight leggings until the door slams and cuts off my view. I consider following her, but my phone is still ringing. I check the screen. Lyric is calling.

I'll deal with Olivia and what just happened later. My boss is more important.

Chapter 11

Foot massage – can feel pretty good but is not better than sex

❧

I'M SITTING AT THE reception desk of *Earth Bliss* working on a business plan when the bell above the door chimes. I look up as Aspen waddles inside. She settles into a chair across from me with a long groan.

"Are you okay?"

"I'm a gazillion months pregnant."

I giggle. "Is that your answer?"

"Trust me. It's the correct answer."

I notice how swollen her feet are. "Dang, girl. Those look painful."

"You don't know the half of it. I don't recommend pregnancy. Zero stars."

I make my way around the reception desk to settle on my knees in front of her.

"What are you doing?"

I waggle my eyebrows. "Not what you think."

"Darn. I never did get a chance to experiment in college since I was with Lyric the entire time."

"You were? I thought you and Lyric only get married last year."

I may not have lived in Colorado for the past two years. And I may have been ignoring my family for the most part. But they still managed to provide me with the gossip highlight reel. Elizabeth thought I'd be intrigued by this wacky town. She wasn't wrong.

"We got lost for a while there."

I nod. I know everything about getting lost.

"Can I remove your sandals?"

"As long as you put them back on. I haven't seen my feet in years. Lyric's been shaving my legs for the past month."

"Why the hell do you bother?" I ask as I remove her sandals.

"No comments about smelly feet. Promise."

I raise three fingers in the girl scout salute, although I'm not technically a girl scout. You rip the arms of your shirt off one time to make a sleeveless top and they lose their minds. Geesh. Talk about an overreaction.

"I promise," I say before beginning to massage her feet.

She moans. "Oh, my god. I think I love you."

"At least someone in this town does," I mutter.

"Who doesn't love you? You're very loveable."

"You're only sweet on me because I'm massaging your feet."

She grunts. "True. But everyone in town seems to be embracing you." She motions to the yoga studio. "Cayenne wants you to take over her business."

"Which is not going to happen if Peace has his way."

"Oh crapadoodle. I forgot why I came here. Pregnancy brain strikes again."

Aspen offered to help me figure out how to win the town over, so I can acquire *Earth Bliss* despite Peace's protests. She claims she has a plan. Considering her sandals don't match, I'm not convinced.

"It's okay. I think I might be a lost cause."

"Hogwash! You need to have faith. Peace protested the twins launching a brewery in town for nearly a year. Guess what? We have a brewery now."

"Why did he protest the brewery?" Does he hate all newcomers? Maybe I'm not special. Although, I felt pretty special when he shoved his tongue down my throat. He tasted of danger and I couldn't get enough.

"Hold on. Why are you blushing?"

What? Am I blushing? I can't be. I don't blush thinking about a man's kiss. Oh wait. Maybe *New and Improved Olivia* does. Not good. I have light skin. I can't get away with blushing without anyone noticing.

"It's hot in here."

Lame. Totally lame.

Aspen snorts. "Even I know it's not hot in here and I'm a trillion years pregnant."

Dang. She's right. Except for during Bikram yoga classes, Cayenne prefers to keep the studio on the cooler side of the spectrum. She tried to explain some agreement she made with the town about energy use, but she lost me at biomass power plant.

"Can we not discuss this?"

She throws her head back and laughs and laughs. Her belly jiggles and she holds onto it as she continues to laugh.

I huff. "What's so funny?"

She points at me. "You! Thinking I'll ever drop a subject."

"Fine." I look around to make sure we're alone. I don't know why we wouldn't be since no one else is in the yoga studio – ever since I told Cayenne I'm interested in assuming management of the studio she's made herself scarce – but precautions are necessary before I admit, "Peace and I kissed."

"You kissed? Tongues and all?"

"Do you really need to know if tongues were involved?"

"Answering a question with a question means the answer is yes. Awesome." She rubs her hands together. "I'm winning Project Opposites."

"Project Opposites?"

"Never you mind."

I stop massaging her feet. "I guess I'm done with your massage."

"Fine. Fine." She shoves her feet at me. "Project Opposites is the name the gossip gals gave to their project to matchmake you with Peace."

What? "They told me they weren't going to matchmake us anymore."

She snorts. "I bet they said you were too different for each other."

"How did you know?"

"We read *In Bed With Mr. Wrong* for book club last month."

"There's a book club in town?" Wait. There is a bigger picture question here. "You read a smutty book for book club?"

"Oh girl. We always read smutty books."

"Hold on. Hold on. Let's backtrack. What does your book club reading a smutty book have to do with the gossip gals?"

"Who do you think picks the books?"

"You. You're the owner of the bookstore."

"Nope. Feather is the picker of books, the purveyor of romance, and the relisher of smut."

"I don't know if I want to join the book club or run far, far away."

"Oh, you're joining. You don't have a choice."

"I don't have a choice?"

"You knew *In Bed With Mr. Wrong* was smutty. You obviously read it. Readers join book club."

"Maybe I guessed it was smutty by the title."

"You're cute."

I grasp at the chance to change the subject and wag my eyebrows at her. "Still regretting the whole not getting a chance to experiment during college thing?"

She sticks out her bottom lip and pouts. "It is unfair."

I chuckle as I massage her feet. Her ankles are pretty much non-existent, so I rub those as well.

She moans. "This is seriously better than sex."

"I'm going to tell Lyric what you said."

"I don't care."

Her eyes fall closed, and she melts into the chair as I work my thumbs into her calves. Wetness trickles down her leg.

I shift away from her. "Um, Aspen? Did you wet yourself?"

"Wet myself? Why would you think I wet myself? Your massage was good, but it wasn't wet myself good."

I indicate the moisture on her legs.

"Oh crap. I wet myself."

I offer her my arm. "Let me help you to the bathroom."

I heave her to her feet and water gushes down her legs.

"I don't think I wet myself this time."

"Nope. Your water broke."

"Lyric is going to kill me. After Ashlyn had her baby on the floor of *Glitter N Bliss*, he made me promise to tell him the second I feel the first contraction."

As much as I want to hear about Ashlyn having her baby on the floor, I need to reassure Aspen who's pressing a shaky palm to her chest. Panic is not good for a woman going into labor.

"Not everyone feels contractions before their water breaks."

"What do you know about it?" She sneers.

"I'm certified in pregnancy yoga. You have to pass a ton of tests."

At my explanation, her shoulders relax and her hands drop to her sides. "Huh. There's more to Oliva Dempsey than the troublemaker."

"Which is what I've been trying to tell everyone," I grumble.

"Here." I lead her to the sofa. "Let's get you comfortable while I phone Lyric."

She lays on her back, but I help to roll to her side. "You shouldn't lay on your back when in the early stages of labor. It can affect the blood supply to the baby."

"You're the labor guru. You should come to the hospital with me."

"I'm pretty sure the nurses and doctors in the hospital know a shedload more than me." I study her. "You good? I'm going to contact Lyric."

She waves me away. "Are you serious? Of course, I'm good. I was ready to meet my baby months ago."

I walk as calmly as I can to my office, but as soon as I'm out of sight of Aspen, I rush to my phone. Lesson learned. Always keep my phone at hand when meeting with a pregnant woman.

"Hello," Lyric answers on the second ring.

"Aspen's in labor. *Earth Bliss* now. Hurry."

I hang up before he can respond. I inhale a few cleansing breaths before returning to the reception area where Aspen is now panting.

I fall to my knees in front of her. "You okay?"

"I think I'm having contractions."

I grasp her hand and squeeze. "You got this. You can't wait to see your baby, remember?"

Her nails bite into my skin as she grunts. "Yes. Baby. Soon."

The door slams open and Lyric rushes in. Phew. I scooch out of his way.

Chapter 12

Olivia the mysterious* *Olivia claims not to have any part in the naming of her as mysterious

❧

PEACE

"Argh!" Lyric shouts and I glance over in time to watch him slam face first into his office door.

"You need to open the door first, boss!" I shout.

He fiddles with the door for a few seconds before kicking it open and charging into the hallway. What the hell? This is not normal behavior for our Chief of Police.

"What's going on?"

His arms flap in the air and his eyes dart around the room. "Aspen. Baby."

"Do I need to phone River?" In addition to being Lyric's brother, River is the town paramedic.

"Yes. No. I don't know."

"Where is she?" I ask as I dial River.

"*Earth Bliss.*"

I grit my teeth. Of all the places for her to be. Olivia will be no help to Aspen. I quickly inform River of the situation before herding Lyric toward the door.

"Come on! Let's go! Aspen needs you!"

We race out of the police station and down Main Street to the yoga studio. I rush inside prepared for a crisis and instead find Aspen laying on her side on a sofa in the reception area while Olivia comforts her. As soon as she notices us, she stands to make way for Lyric.

"What should we do?" Lyric asks.

Aspen giggles. "You're asking me? Aren't you the one who read the pregnancy book five times?"

"It wasn't five times."

She rolls her eyes. "Then, you weren't hiding in the bathroom with a copy while you pretended to be constipated?"

Olivia laughs and my gaze finds hers. Her humor disappears when she notices me. To her credit, however, she doesn't flee. She straightens her back and marches to me.

"Her water broke." She checks her watch. "Five minutes ago and she's had two contractions since then. I didn't time them but they were several minutes apart."

"Um…" I'm unsure why she's informing me. Does she think I know how to deliver a baby? Sure, we had a class on childbirth during the academy, but there's no way I'm delivering Aspen's baby. Especially since I don't remember a thing from the class at the moment.

River dashes into the building and I breathe a sigh of relief. He can handle this. He nods at me before rushing to his sister-in-law and brother.

"Aspen, Aspen," he tuts as he dons gloves. "Just because I delivered your sister's baby doesn't mean I want to deliver yours."

"But I can't let Ashlyn beat me."

"The Wests. Always so competitive."

Lyric growls. "You know damn well her name is Alston now."

River winks at Aspen. "He's too easy."

She giggles before she groans and clutches her stomach. "Effing ouch."

Olivia hurries forward. "How can I help? I have blankets if you need them. Cushions, too. And you can use my office if you want some privacy."

"Privacy?" Olivia indicates the window and Aspen's eyes widen when she notices the crowd gathering on the sidewalk outside of the studio.

"My car is parked in the alley," Olivia says in a loud voice to draw Aspen's attention away from the crowd. "You're welcome to use it."

I step forward. "I can put down some blankets on the back seat. Just in case."

She waves me away. "Whatever. It doesn't matter."

Is she serious? Her car is worth more than I earn in a year. Probably two years. She should take better care of her things. Although, I bet the car is Beckett's and not hers, anyway.

"It's more important we ensure Aspen has a healthy baby. I can always get the upholstery steamed later."

Damn. Maybe she's not being selfish. Maybe she's more worried about Aspen than her car. And maybe I was wrong about her. Nah. I'm not wrong.

Mrs. West rushes inside. "What is it with my daughters? I taught them better about when to know they're in labor."

Aspen waves at her mom. "Are you ready to be a grandmother?"

"I have two grandchildren already or have you forgotten about Ellery's baby girl and Ashlyn's baby girl?"

"But I'm the oldest and your favorite."

"It's wrong to have favorites."

"Um. I hate to interrupt this discussion, but shouldn't we worry about getting Aspen to the hospital?" Olivia motions toward the rear entrance. "My car."

"What should I do?" Lyric asks River. "Can she make it to the hospital?"

"I need to see how far she's dilated."

"Get on with it."

River cocks a brow. "You do realize I need to examine your wife's private regions?"

Olivia pushes her way in between them. "Grab Lyric," she orders me. "Here." She hands Mrs. West a blanket. "Protect your daughter's privacy. I'm going to lock the door before anyone else rushes in here."

I clamp a hand around Lyric's wrist while Aspen's mom holds the blanket up and River ducks under it.

"I bet you've had lots of experience ducking your head under blankets before," Aspen teases.

Lyric growls and I have to wrap my arms around his middle to stop him from attacking River. "Easy, brother. She's not serious."

River peeks out from underneath the blanket. He waggles his eyebrows. "There's only one woman's blanket I duck under now."

Olivia growls. "You better be referring to my sister, Elizabeth."

"He is," Mrs. West answers.

"I'm sorry. We haven't met." Olivia reaches her hand out before she realizes Mrs. West doesn't have a hand to give her. She waves instead. "I'm Olivia. Elizabeth is my sister."

"I know. You're the mysterious Olivia."

Olivia snorts. "There's nothing mysterious about me."

I have to disagree. Olivia the criminal wouldn't be standing here joking with people while calmly making certain Aspen is taken care of.

"Oh, there's something mysterious about you all right," Mrs. West responds to Olivia, but her gaze is stuck on me.

Great. Another nosy woman. This town has more than its fair share. I wouldn't be surprised if Mrs. West joined the gossip gals. She's probably drafting her application form in her head as we speak.

River reaches up and removes the blanket. "She's hardly dilated. You should make it to the hospital in White Bridge without any problems."

Olivia rushes into her office and returns dangling her keys. "Who's driving?"

Lyric raises his hand, but I snag the keys before he can. "You need to stay in the backseat with your wife."

"Do you need help carrying her to the car?" Olivia asks Lyric.

"Carrying me? I'm perfectly capable of walking," Aspen claims before trying to stand. Her legs wobble and Lyric and Olivia rush to her before she can fall.

"Maybe let your big, strong husband carry you," Olivia suggests. "After all, it's his fault you're in this condition."

Lyric groans. "Thanks for reminding her."

"I'm pretty sure she doesn't need a reminder."

"I'm walking," Aspen insists.

Lyric grasps one arm while Olivia grasps the other and together they help her to hobble through the studio to the backdoor.

"Oh no, Olivia. I'm getting your floor dirty."

Olivia laughs. "Don't worry. I have a mop and I know how to use it."

My brow furrows. Olivia cleans? I wouldn't expect her to lower herself to manual tasks. *You don't know her very well, do you?* A voice whispers in the back of my mind. Crap. Was Olivia right? Did I judge her too quickly?

Olivia's fancy electric car is parked in the alley. As soon as I'm near, the locks beep open. I hold the back door open for Aspen and Lyric while River rushes around to the passenger seat and gets in.

Once Aspen is settled, I slam the door.

"I'll bring the car back as soon as I can," I tell Olivia.

"It's no rush. I'll find another ride home. Take care of Aspen."

I nod before sliding into the driver's seat. I press a button and the engine purrs to life. Maybe I won't be returning this car as soon as I can, after all.

Olivia knocks on the window and I roll it down.

"The registration is in the glove compartment and the battery should be full, so you don't need to worry about finding a charging station."

She shoves a paper bag at me. "Some snacks and drinks. Food at hospitals is gross and you may be there a while."

My mouth gapes open. Is she taking care of me? After everything I've said and done to her? Damn. I did misjudge her. I clear my throat and prepare myself to force the words 'thank you' out, but she waves at me.

"Get going. Aspen probably wants drugs for the pain relief."

"Drugs! I want all the drugs!" Aspen screams from the backseat.

I use the distraction to roll the window up and drive away without having to say thank you. I'll thank her later. After I spend some time trying to figure out who this mysterious woman is. Because there's more to Olivia than her criminal record.

Chapter 13

❧

"I GUESS YOU HAVEN'T talked to Cassandra yet."

I frown at Elizabeth. She's not wrong, but she could give me a break in the whole Cassandra versus Olivia debate for one freaking day. We're supposed to be having fun here. Not analyzing everything I've ever done wrong in my life. There's not enough time in the world to analyze all my faults.

"I don't know what you're referring to."

I'm also a big, fat liar. Witness me scratching my neck as proof. There's a festival in Winter Falls today, and I asked Elizabeth and Gabrielle if they wanted to go with me. Obviously, I didn't ask Cassandra.

Our communication is still limited to sending each other emojis. But there is progress. Cassie sent me a gif – a person being humped by a dog while performing yoga – on her own initiative.

I had hoped Cassandra's absence wouldn't be remarked up. My hope was in vain.

"Have you met little Sterling yet?" I ask in a blatant attempt to change the subject.

"Aspen's baby boy is adorable, but I'm not allowing you to change the subject. If you think I'm not going to do everything in my power to make sure the two of you kiss and make up, you're wrong."

Gabrielle giggles and I glare down at her. She holds up her hands. "Elizabeth's not wrong. You and Cassie need to figure things out."

My glare turns into a scowl, but I'm merely playing. It's nice to see Gabrielle come out of her shell. When she left Saint Louis two years ago, she was a mess. I couldn't be more thankful to Phoenix for loving her and returning my sister to me.

"What's this Mabon festival about anyway?" I ask in another blatant attempt to change the subject.

Trust me. I have a ton of ideas on how to change the subject. Someone's had a bunch of experience in avoiding topics she doesn't want to discuss.

Elizabeth narrows her eyes on me, but Gabrielle doesn't hesitate to answer. "It's a festival to celebrate the harvest."

"And what kinds of activities are there?"

Elizabeth waves her arm toward Main Street, which is packed with tourists. I could hardly believe it when I drove toward town and ended up in traffic. Traffic! In Winter Falls? The town where driving a car – even if it is electric – causes people to wag their fingers at you? Shocking!

"There's apple wine tasting, an apple pie contest, and a stacking applies contest," Elizabeth explains.

"Plus, all of the stores have booths set up to sell their wares," Gabrielle adds.

"My apple pie is going to win this year," I hear someone shout.

"As if your pie could ever beat my man's!"

Elizabeth drags me toward the voices.

"*Bake Me Happy*," I read the sign above the store. "There's a bakery in Winter Falls?"

"Yep! And it's the best bakery in Colorado," Ashlyn announces.

"And yet I'm going to win the apple pie contest this year," a familiar-looking woman says.

"You remember Moon?" Elizabeth asks. "Ashlyn's best friend?"

Ah, yes. Now I remember her.

"Some best friend Ashlyn is when she doesn't support my dreams," Moon complains.

"What do you mean?" I ask because curious is my middle name when it comes to Winter Falls.

"There's an annual apple pie contest during the Mabon festival. I've been trying to win for years," Moon begins. "I want to be a baker and open my own bakery."

Ashlyn huffs. "And I keep explaining to her this town is not big enough for two bakeries."

Moon points at her. "This is exactly what I mean. My best friend doesn't support my dreams."

"Where is this pie?" I interrupt to ask. "Can I try some?"

Moon threads her arm through mine. "You're my new best friend."

Ashlyn grasps hold of my other arm. "I already claimed her as my new best friend. You can't have her."

Moon yanks me toward her. "I was first."

Ashlyn yanks me back. "No! I was first!"

Rowan exits the bakery, takes one look at the two women using me as rope in their tug-of-war contest, and huffs before marching forward and claiming his wife.

"Dream girl," he mutters as he kisses her hair.

"She insists her apple pie is better than yours," Ashlyn responds as if it's an excuse for playing tug-of-war with a person.

"Moon's apple pie is pretty good." He lifts his chin toward Moon. "When are you going to come work for me?"

She frowns. "I'm not stupid. I'm not working for my best friend's husband. It's a recipe for disaster."

Ashlyn giggles. "She said recipe."

I groan. "Will everyone stop mentioning pie when I'm starving?"

Moon jerks my arm. "Come on. I'll accompany you to the pie contest area."

I wave to Ashlyn and Rowan as we set off.

"You better vote for Rowan's pie, Olivia! Or I'm going to tell everyone you're not my sister."

"You aren't my sister."

"Yes, I am! You're related to Cassandra who's living with my husband's brother. See? Sisters."

I chuckle. "Someone didn't pass biology class."

"Welcome to the pie eating contest!" Moon announces as we reach the town square.

I scan the area and my eyes widen when I notice table after table laden with apple pie. "Do I have to try each of these?"

"Don't be silly. Just one slice from each table."

I quickly count the tables. "There are ten tables. You expect me to eat ten different slices of pie?"

"We'll help," Elizabeth volunteers.

"And after we finish eating apple pie, we can try some apple wine." Gabrielle points to a booth claiming to have ten different varieties of apple wine to taste.

"I'm going to gain twenty pounds today."

"Good thing you teach yoga for a living," Gabrielle says.

I frown at her. Is she digging at me for not explaining to her what I do for a living? When she reaches forth and squeezes my hand, I realize I'm jumping to conclusions.

Speaking of jumping to conclusions, I catch sight of Peace prowling toward me. I've managed to avoid the sexy cop since Aspen went into labor in *Earth Bliss.* I was out doing errands when he returned the car. Lucky me.

Peace stops smack dab in front of me. It appears as if my luck has run out.

"Officer."

"Ms. Dempsey."

My sisters slink away. "Hey! Where are you two going?"

Elizabeth winks at me, while Gabrielle gives me a thumbs-up. Some wing women those two are.

"Can I speak to you?"

"You may," I snark because I am trying to be the *New and Improved Olivia*, but *Past Olivia* will never completely disappear.

To my surprise, Peace chuckles. But then his eyes widen and he captures my wrist before hauling me away.

"What are you doing?" I struggle against his hold. "I didn't commit a crime. You can't arrest me because you hate me."

I must be faint from hunger because I swear he mumbles, "I wish I hated you."

He clears his throat. "The gossip gals are chasing us."

I glance over my shoulder. I nearly stumble when I see the five elderly women clamoring after us. Sage is holding up a camera and snapping pictures.

"What are they doing?"

"Being nosy busybodies."

I giggle. I can't help it. "This is ridiculous. Those women will never catch us. There's no reason to run."

He leads me into an alley before slowing down.

"Now we can have a conversation without any interruptions."

He begins rubbing circles on my wrist and I forget all about how this man hates me. How he thinks I'm the scum of the earth. All I can think about is how good it feels to have his thumb touch my bare skin. How good he tasted when his tongue invaded my mouth.

"Olivia?"

I yank my hand away from his hold. "Yes?"

He glances down at my hand and frowns. "We need to talk."

If he's here to apologize for our kiss, I'm going to kill him. I don't care if he's a cop. He's dead.

"You've repeated yourself three times now. Maybe it's time to actually start talking."

He runs a hand through his hair. I wish I was the one with my hands in his hair. I bet it feels soft as silk. Too bad I didn't get my hands on it when we kissed. I clasp my hands together before I can do anything supremely stupid such as check for myself how soft his hair feels.

"I need to apologize."

Past Olivia gets the shovel out. *It's time for the pig to die.*

"I may have judged you before getting to know you."

I couldn't be more surprised if he announced he's an alien from Mars and he's been sent to Earth to rid the planet of all evildoers and I'm his first victim. My mouth drops open.

"Are you serious?"

He can't be. In my experience, cops never apologize. Even if they arrest you for being in the wrong place at the wrong time while doing nothing wrong. Assuming being overly drunk and swearing at the police while making rude gestures isn't technically wrong.

"I think they're in here," Feather says and Peace shifts to cover me so the women won't see me.

Uh oh. This is bad. Peace towers over me and his chest heaves as it moves against mine. My nipples harden at the feel of those hard muscles.

Past Olivia drops her shovel. She's ready to rip his clothes off and have her wicked way with him. My stomach tingles. *New and Improved Olivia* wouldn't mind getting a taste of him either.

His gaze drops to my mouth and my tongue peeks out to lick my bottom lip. He groans.

"Fuck it," he mumbles and then his lips are on mine.

New and Improved Olivia takes a hike and *Past Olivia* takes over. I thread my hands through his hair – it's as soft as I'd hoped – and pull him close as my tongue duels with his.

Hell yeah.

Chapter 14

Tangled sheets – won't be happening anytime soon

❧

PEACE

Olivia's lips taste even better than I remember and I remember them tasting pretty fucking fantastic. Her tongue tries to invade my mouth, but I growl before tilting her head to my liking and showing her who's in charge of this kiss.

I grasp her leg and throw it around my waist. I groan when her leg tightens around me. I want to feel her legs wrapped around me while I pound into her. My cock twitches at the idea and I punch my hips forward. She moans as my hard length rubs against her center.

"Excellent!"

I wrench my lips from Olivia's and turn to glare at the group of gossip gals who are standing at the end of the alley watching us.

"Don't mind us," Sage hollers.

"We won't interrupt," Feather adds.

"Please continue. I'm taking notes for Sirius." I'll be damned. Clove is seriously writing in a small notepad.

I don't bother to respond to their crazy. I'm a police officer. I know there is no response to crazy.

I return my attention to Olivia. I smirk when I notice her lips are swollen and her hair is mussed. I tuck a strand of her silky blonde locks behind her ear.

"Let's continue this somewhere private."

She freezes. "I'm not... It's... I mean... You are..."

Crap. There I go making assumptions again.

"We don't need to do anything. We can stick to talking." I nod toward the gossip gals who are trying to sneak closer to listen. "Without them overhearing."

"What did you say?" Feather shouts.

"I can't hear them. Can you?" Cayenne grumbles.

Olivia scowls. "You agreed not to match me with Peace."

"I lied," Cayenne says. "It was for your own good."

Olivia huffs. "I should have listened when Aspen started talking about *In Bed With Mr. Wrong.* I didn't and now I'm paying the price."

I chuckle. "I'm confused. In bed with Mr. Wrong?"

"Never you mind, Mr. Steal A Kiss."

I waggle my eyebrows. "Is it stealing when you participated wholeheartedly?"

"I rate it nine peppers," Petal declares.

"You can't give a kiss nine peppers. The scale is from one to five," Sage says.

"I stick by my initial rating. He looked ready to rip her clothes off. Nine peppers."

"I give them eight," Clove says and Sage groans. "Their clothes are entirely intact."

Feather points at Sage. "If you hadn't yelled excellent, clothes would have come off."

Olivia drops her leg from around my waist and tries to scooch away from them, but I'm not letting her escape. We need to talk now more than ever.

I grasp her hand and step away from her. "Come on. Let's go find your sisters."

At the suggestion of finding her sisters, the tension in her shoulders releases and she nods before her gaze drops to the ground.

I don't have time to question her sudden shyness when the gossip gals are quickly approaching.

"Let the chase begin." I wink before leading her out of the alley to the street parallel to Main.

She giggles as I pretend to flee the gossip gals. My gaze darts from side to side as I feign terror at being followed. I clench her hand.

"I think we lost them," I whisper when we turn left toward the square.

She bursts out laughing. And here I thought she was beautiful when she was scowling at me. When her face is full of happiness, she's gorgeous – practically irresistible.

My hands itch to rove over her body while my mouth explores hers. My desire must show on my face because the smile drops from her face and she steps away. I drop her hand.

"I don't know what's happening here, but you need to know I would never pressure you to do anything you don't want to."

"I know. It's not you. It's me."

I groan. Those words signal the end of our beginning.

"Let me return you to your family. We can forget this ever happened."

"Forget this happened?" Her brow wrinkles as she studies me. "Is that what you want? To forget our incredible kiss?"

I smirk. "Incredible?"

"Damn," she mutters before slamming a hand over her mouth.

"It's okay." I waggle my eyebrows. "I won't let your adoration of my kisses go to my head."

She giggles as her hands drop. "I think it already did."

"Okay. We're agreed. I give the best kisses and we won't forget about it?" I add a question mark to the last sentence because I'm confused.

She was into the kiss. I know she was. You can't fake the kind of passion we have. But she doesn't want to go any further.

She rolls her eyes. "I'm not going to forget about our kiss. It happened less than five minutes ago. My memory is perfectly intact."

"But you don't want to go any further?" I push.

"I do want to go further, which is the problem," she mutters.

My confusion must show on my face because she sighs before grasping my hand and drawing me toward the alley behind *Clove's Coffee Chop.* She keeps going until we reach *Earth Bliss.* She unlocks the back door and ushers me in.

"This is beyond embarrassing," she says as she wrings her hands.

I clasp her hands and pry them apart. "You can tell me anything."

She snorts. "I can? You hated me before you got your tongue down my throat."

I chuckle. The woman has a way with words. "I didn't hate you."

She raises her eyebrows and meets my gaze full on. This is not a woman you can ever bullshit. She won't let you get away with it.

I tuck a strand of hair behind her ear. "I could never hate you."

She slaps my chest. "You weren't exactly nice to me when we first met. In fact, until our lips clashed, you weren't nice to me at all."

I capture her hand to keep it against my chest. "I was an asshole."

Her nose scrunches. "Does this mean you expect me to admit to being a bitch? Because I won't."

I glance down when I realize her hand is now caressing my chest. When she realizes what she's doing, she whips her hand away.

"I don't want to have sex with you," she blurts out.

"What?"

"I mean. I do. Want to have sex that is. With you. But not at this very m-m-moment." She clears her throat. "I do want to have sex with you now, but I don't. I mean I can't. I mean I shouldn't."

I cup her face in my palms. "Take a breath, trouble. No one's having sex right now."

"You don't want to have sex with me?"

"Darling, every man who catches a glimpse of you wants to have sex with you."

She winks. "I know."

"But we can take things slow."

"We can? I mean…" She clears her throat. "I want to take things slow."

She fiddles with the hem of her t-shirt and I wait her out. She obviously has more to say, but I won't push her. I've been an asshole enough to her.

"I have a bad habit," she admits to the floor. "I have a tendency to jump to the physical part of a relationship before getting to know someone." She glances up at me from beneath her eyelashes. "I want to get to know you more before we have sex."

I pinch her chin and use my hold to lift her head until she meets my gaze.

"I'm sorry I suggested we have sex before you were ready."

"I think I'm going to dub you Mr. Apology. First, you couldn't be a big enough asshole. And, now, you're being Mr. Sweet. Which one is the real Peace?"

"I guess you're going to have to get to know me to find out." I wink. "Starting with a date. Would you, Ms. Olivia Dempsey, like to accompany me to movie night this week?"

"Yes, Mr. Peace … Wait. What's your last name?"

"Sky."

"Yes, Mr. Peace Sky." She giggles and I glare. "Sorry. Sorry. You have to admit it's a funny name."

"This is Winter Falls. Everyone's name is funny."

"True. I met a man named Forest who walks his squirrels half naked."

I'm familiar with Forest. He owns the pet store, *Unleashed,* two stores down. And he hates pants. Even in the deep of winter, he hates wearing them. And underwear. He lets it all hang out.

"Now, we've settled all our burning issues, let's return to the Mabon festival."

I lead her out of the yoga studio onto Main Street where several people are strolling up and down with apples piled on top of their heads.

"What are they doing?" Olivia asks as she points to the group.

"Hey, Olivia! I'm winning!" Elizabeth calls before tripping and tumbling toward the ground. She hits Gabrielle on her way and the two end up sprawled on the ground.

"Best fall goes to Elizabeth Dempsey!" Eden announces and Elizabeth cheers from her spot in the middle of the street.

"Hey!" Gabrielle huffs as she gets to her feet. "She fell on me. Don't I get a consolation prize?"

"You can have one of my pies," Moon hollers. "They're the best in town."

Olivia laughs. "This town is crazy."

"Admit it. You love it."

She grins up at me. I want to kiss those pink lips again, but I know better. I tweak her nose instead.

I can admit – even if it's only to myself – I'm excited to see where things with Olivia will go. I'm not convinced she isn't trouble, but she might be the right kind of trouble. The kind of trouble that ends in twisted sheets and sweaty bodies.

Chapter 15

Flirty banter – way more fun than throwing barbs at each other

❧

I'VE NEVER BEEN THIS nervous about a date before. Truth be told, I haven't been on many dates. I may have been a bit promi—

Nope. I'm not going to rehash all the reasons why *Past Olivia* is being transformed into *New and Improved Olivia*. No one wants to hear about my past. Least of all, me.

I repeat my mantra. *I am present in this moment.*

I end up repeating the mantra five times before I manage to open the car door. I approach the library where Peace stands at the entrance waiting for me. I can see the smirk on his face from here. Is he making fun of my inability to get out of my car?

What am I doing? A cop is not the type of man I should want to get to know better. It seems my body doesn't care what my head is thinking as my legs carry me to him.

"Hi, trouble," Peace whispers before kissing my cheek. His lips touch my skin and I forget all about why I shouldn't want to be involved with a lawman.

"Hi, Johnny Law."

He chuckles as he grasps my hand and leads me inside. The library is crowded when we enter. It appears the whole town is here, but I don't catch sight of any of my sisters.

"Is it always this busy?" I ask as I glance around.

He waggles his eyebrows. "We can always sneak into the stacks if the crowd is too much for you."

I widen my eyes and clutch my non-existent pearls. "Why, Mr. Officer? Are you suggesting a sexual bribe?"

My lips tingle in anticipation. I want to be in those stacks with him. Screw the movie.

Before he can carry me away, Ashlyn starts singing, "Peace and Olivia sitting in a tree. K-i-s-s-i-n-g."

"How old are you?" Peace grumbles.

She wiggles her eyebrows. "Old enough to know this night will not end with kissing."

I cringe. This night should end with kissing. I want to get to know Peace before I jump into bed with him. It's a novelty for me, but I'm trying.

"Dream girl," Rowan mutters before hauling her away.

"I wasn't doing anything wrong."

Juniper bustles our way. "You made it!"

She herds us toward the front of the room where there's an empty loveseat. "Sit. Sit. I saved you a spot."

"Saving them a spot doesn't mean you'll win the bet," Mrs. West hollers.

"Already won ten bucks, though, didn't I?" Juniper addresses me. "Everyone else said you were too chicken to show."

Peace whistles loud enough for everyone to hear him. "Can everyone cool it with the bets?" he asks when everyone's attention is on him. It's not a question. It's clearly a demand. My stomach warms. I do enjoy a demanding man.

Lilac nods. "I agree, but when I brought it to a vote before the town, I lost."

"Lilac Bean West," Mrs. West harrumphs.

"Soon to be Dempsey," Beckett interrupts to correct.

I wave to him. "Hey, big bro."

He winks at me before pointing at Peace. "I've got my eyes on you."

He needs to cool it with the big brother act, but Lilac speaks before I have the chance to tell him to back off. "Why am I getting the middle name treatment?" she asks her mom.

"A little harmless betting never hurt anyone."

"Harmless and betting don't necessarily go together. In fact—"

Juniper claps her hands to gain everyone's attention. "Why don't we roll the film before Lilac begins one of her lectures about the risks of becoming addicted to gambling?"

A shout goes up from the back of the room. "Here! Here!"

I glance behind me to find the gossip gals sitting together around a table. They send me winks and thumbs-ups. I sigh. I should have known they'd be here.

"What film are we watching?" Ashlyn asks.

"I bet I know," Mrs. West says.

Ashlyn rubs her hands together. "I'll take your bet!"

"Dream girl, you already lost ten dollars to Juniper."

She rolls her eyes at her husband. "I think we can afford to lose ten dollars. You could shut the bakery and I could close the recording studio and we'd still be living comfortably for the rest of our lives."

"Ashlyn owns a recording studio?" I whisper my question to Peace.

"Yep. You've probably heard of it. *Bertie's Recording Studio.* Ashlyn's a well-known audiobook narrator."

My mouth gapes open. "You're kidding."

"Hey!" Ashlyn is suddenly standing right in front of me. For someone who enjoys making a fuss wherever she goes, she can be stealthy when she wants to be. "Do you think I couldn't be well-known?"

"No. No. No." No one knows better than me to not judge people. "I'm surprised you have time to record audiobooks is all. You have a lot on your plate."

"Don't worry. I'm wonder woman." She places her hands on her hips, juts out her chest, and lifts her chin.

"Is this your wonder woman pose?"

Her nose wrinkles. "I'll work on it." She tromps back to her loveseat where Rowan's waiting.

Juniper claps her hands to gain everyone's attention again. I raise my hand. She huffs before pointing at me. "Yes?"

"Do you actually watch a film on movie night?"

Peace laughs next to me before wrapping an arm around my shoulders and settling us into the loveseat. "Be careful. You don't want to throw down against the West sisters."

"I don't?"

Past Olivia could eat the West Sisters for breakfast and be hungry by brunch. *You're not Past Olivia anymore, remember?* Oh yeah.

"Tonight's movie is…" Juniper pauses for dramatic purposes. "*The Ugly Truth.*"

"Ha! I knew it! You owe me, Mom," Ashlyn says.

"I was sure the movie would be *Two Weeks Notice*," Mrs. West complains.

"Is the movie not announced in advance?" I ask Peace.

"Juniper enjoys surprising everyone."

"Then, how did Ashlyn guess the movie?"

He squirms. I pinch his side. "Tell me before the tickle assault begins."

"What if I'm not ticklish?"

"I'll begin a pinching assault."

He holds up his hands in surrender. "I give. I give."

"I haven't even begun to torture you yet."

He leans close to whisper in my ear. "Oh, but you have, trouble. You have."

Now it's my turn to squirm in my seat. A man's breath flowing over my ear has always been a hot spot for me. "Back atcha, JL."

"JL?"

"Johnny Law. Duh."

His gaze dips to my lips and I wonder if the option to sneak off to the stacks is still on the table. I bite my lip and he groans.

A popcorn kernel lands on my shirt. "No making out at the movies," Beckett commands.

His comment has me inching away from Peace. Kissing him in front of my brother is not a good idea. *Why not? Past Olivia* asks but I ignore her.

"Tell me how Ashlyn guessed the name of the film."

"It's Winter Falls."

I wiggle my fingers before reaching for his waist. He shackles my wrist to stop me. Someone must be ticklish. I file the information away for future use.

"Everyone knows everything. There are no secrets in town."

"Continue," I push when he pauses.

"Meaning everyone knew you and I would be here tonight on a date."

I'm not surprised. I told Gabrielle and Elizabeth about my date and those two are notorious for their inability to keep a secret. What does surprise me is their absence. I figured they'd be here to witness the date for themselves.

"What does this have to do with the film?"

"*The Ugly Truth? Two Weeks Notice?* What do they both have in common?"

I'm obviously missing the clue here. "They're older romantic comedies."

"The characters in both movies are opposites."

I put the clues together. "We're opposites. This movie was chosen because of us."

"And they bet on it," he adds.

This is not the first time someone has mentioned betting. "Is everyone constantly betting in this town?"

"Pretty much."

"And they're betting on us. Whether we get together?" Aspen mentioned the whole gossip gal project to matchmake me with Peace, but she never said anything about bets. "How much do they bet?"

"Why? Do you want in on it?"

"Exactly. We could do a whole fake relationship thing and cash in on the bets."

He frowns. "You want the money."

I roll my eyes. "Not me, JL. We could donate it to charity. I bet the community center could use some funds."

"You'd really donate the money?"

"Yeah. Of course. What else would I do with it? Run off to Hawaii?" My nose wrinkles. "Not worth the hassle."

His back straightens. "What happened in Hawaii?"

I slap his chest. "Nothing, silly. I was kidding."

Now, substitute Hawaii for Alaska and we have a story. A story I have no intention of repeating to anyone ever, although it wasn't my fault. Someone could have warned me how fast snowmobiles can go.

The lights dim, and Peace hands me a bucket of popcorn. "Where did this come from?"

"The same place this did." He hands me a beer.

"I'm driving."

"Which is why it's non-alcoholic. But I have normal beer if you prefer. Or a pop."

I lean over him to check out where all his supplies are coming from. There's a shopping bag stuffed full of drinks next to his seat.

"You thought of everything, didn't you?"

"I try."

"Not bad, JL. Not bad."

It's more than not bad. It's pretty awesome. As is Peace. Oh crap. I don't merely have the hots for the cop, I genuinely like him. I need to flee. Hold on. That's *Past Olivia* speaking. She doesn't have decision making privileges anymore.

Nope. *New and Improved Olivia* is going to see where this goes. And enjoy the hell out of it in the meantime. Starting now. I lean into Peace's chest, and he wraps an arm around my shoulders. Good start.

Chapter 16

Stall – a delay tactic that has zero percent chance of success when a cop is involved regardless of how sexy said cop looks in his uniform

✦

"Hi!" I wave at Peace as he exits the courthouse.

I stand mesmerized as he swaggers down the steps. It's becoming clear to me why women find a man in a uniform irresistible because Peace is h-a-w-t in his police outfit. The t-shirt stretches over his chest offering me a glimpse of those hard muscles beneath. And those jeans hugging his thighs? Oh my.

"Good morning, Olivia." He kisses my cheek and my body sways toward him. The feel of his soft lips on my skin and his clean scent makes me want to melt into him.

This is a cop! Past Olivia reminds me.

Cop. Schmop. Did you miss the way his jeans hug his thighs?

"You want to get a coffee at *Clove's Coffee Corner* or *Bake Me Happy*?"

I snort. As if there's any question considering the gossip gals hang out at Clove's. The fact Rowan makes the best apple turnovers has nothing to do with it. "*Bake Me Happy.*"

He grasps my hand and leads me down Main Street toward Rowan's bakery.

"How are things at *Earth Bliss* going?"

"Are we pretending you don't know I have to write a business plan before the town allows me to assume control of the business?"

He frowns. "It's the normal way of doing things."

"Except the town would have rubberstamped me if it weren't for you."

"Do you want me to apologize for being an asshole again?"

I tap my chin as if I'm considering it. "Maybe? And could you get down on your knees while you do it? Maybe remove your shirt?"

"My little troublemaker," he says while shaking his head.

I push up on my toes. "Who you calling little?"

"You, squirt!"

"Squirt?" I raise my hands and wiggle my fingers. "I'll show you!"

"Oh no!" He claps his hands to his cheeks and feigns terror. "Please don't tickle me."

If he thinks I don't know he's ticklish, he's wrong. I tickle his ribs and he laughs as he squirms and dances away from me.

"Do you give?" I chase after him.

"Never!"

"This is even better than I could have dreamed," Sage says and I whirl around to find her standing on the steps of the courthouse watching us.

Peace throws an arm around my shoulders and pulls me near. "Give it a rest."

Sage bats her eyelashes. "Me?" She places a hand over her heart. "I wasn't doing anything."

"If she's innocent, I'm a cow," he grumbles.

"Can you moo like a cow?"

"Moo!"

I giggle. "I didn't think a cop could be playful."

He tweaks my nose. "Don't judge me before you get to know me."

He's one to talk. "Pot. Meet kettle."

He shakes my hand. "Nice to meet you, kettle."

I pump his hand up and down. "You, too, pot."

"I should have brought popcorn."

At Clove's announcement, I sigh.

"I'm in dire need of an apple turnover now."

Peace offers me his arm. "Let's go." I thread my arm through his and he leans over to whisper, "Ignore them. This is small town living."

I frown. I didn't sign on for living in a small town where everyone knows my business. I don't know if small town living is for me.

We stroll to the entrance of *Bake Me Happy*. I grasp the door to enter but freeze when I notice Cassandra sitting at a table inside.

"Maybe this is a bad idea," I mutter before turning around to flee.

Peace catches me before I can make my escape. "What's wrong?"

"Cassandra's in there."

He glances around me. "So she is. Big deal. You're going to have to talk to her at some point."

"I'm not ready."

He whirls me around before pushing me forward. "You're never going to be ready."

I'm such an idiot. Forget about *New and Improved Olivia.* I'm now *Idiot Olivia.* What possessed me to tell Peace it's time for me to make amends with Cassandra? It definitely wasn't post-coital bliss. Ever since I told him I want to hold off on sex, he's treated me with kid gloves.

I plant my feet. "I need more time."

He whispers into my ear. "Are you chicken?"

Of course, I'm chicken! Show me a person who isn't chicken to have a sit down with her sister who is pissed off at her for a good reason.

"I'm not chicken," I lie.

"Really? And you're not lying?"

He snags my hand from where I'm scratching my neck. This is what I get for making friends with a cop. I glance up at Peace from under my lashes. He smirks at me and I want to wipe that smirk clear off his face. With a kiss. And maybe a little biting. And some scratching.

"Cassie isn't going to forgive me anyway. Let's go to *Clove's Coffee Corner* instead."

His hand tightens on mine before he hauls me away. Yeah! I'm winning. No awkward discussions for Olivia today.

But instead of leading me to Clove's place, he turns in the opposite direction toward the community center. He opens a door to one of the private rooms and shoves me inside.

"Why are you afraid to have a discussion with your sister?" he asks after he shuts the door behind him.

"I'm not afraid!"

"Stop lying to me."

I stomp my foot. "I'm not lying."

"Did you forget who I am? I'm a police officer. I know when a person is lying."

I want to snarl at him. In fact, I lift the corner of my lip, but I'm not *Past Olivia*. I'm *New and Improved Olivia. New and Improved Olivia* is not a liar. She doesn't automatically lie to cops because she doesn't trust the establishment.

My shoulders drop and I concentrate on the floor. "Cassie hates me. She's never going to forgive me."

He palms my neck and squeezes. "Livie, your sister doesn't hate you."

I ignore how my chest warms at his use of an endearment for me. Unfortunately, now is not the time to go all gooey over a man.

"Easy for you to say. You don't have any siblings. You don't know how angry they can get."

"Stop lashing out at me."

Ugh! Why am I dating a cop who doesn't hesitate to call me out? Who's idea was this?

"I know you're scared."

I bristle. Olivia Lucy Dempsey is not afraid of anything.

He places his forehead against mine. "It's okay. Everyone gets scared sometimes."

"Oh yeah? When was the last time you were scared?"

"About a week before we met."

"What happened?"

"I caught Sage searching for male strippers online."

This is getting interesting. "Why were you scared?"

"Because she claimed she's going to send me a male stripper for my birthday."

"When's your birthday? I'll ask if she can order the stripper."

He tweaks my nose. "The only man who's going to strip for you on my birthday is me."

I shiver as tingles spark and travel through my body spreading heat. I one-hundred percent support this idea.

His eyes fall shut and he swears under his breath. "I'm sorry. I promised I wouldn't push you to become physical and here I am proposing stripping for you."

I cup his chin and his eyes snap open. "I like the idea. Trust me. I like it a whole lot."

His smile is sad. "It doesn't change how as a man I shouldn't push a woman before she's ready."

My body is ready. Two-hundred and fifty-percent ready to jump him. To taste him. To touch him. My leg lifts, but before I can wrap it around his middle, Peace steps away.

"Back to the discussion at hand."

Discussion at hand? What discussion? Aren't we done talking? Isn't it time to proceed to stripping off clothes and getting hot and sweaty?

"Cassandra will understand if you explain why you ghosted her for the past two years."

His words work better at dampening my libido than a bucket of ice cold water.

"My sister holds a mean grudge."

Last time I checked, she was still mad at me for borrowing her skirt when I was eighteen. It's not as if it's my fault the skirt ended up torn. How was I to know there was a nail on the ledge of the window I was sneaking out of after the police raided the party? I didn't exactly have time to check for obstructions before I dove out of the window.

New and Improved Olivia shakes her head at me. *It's your fault for being at the party,* she claims. Geez. *New and Improved Olivia* sounds awfully similar to Cassandra. Crap. I need to talk to my sister.

"Come on." Peace opens the door. "I'll be sitting behind you the entire time."

"My emotional support police officer."

He waggles his eyebrows. "When duty calls, I answer."

I snatch his hand. "Okay, ESPO. Let's move out."

He chuckles. "You and initials."

We exit the community center and approach the bakery. My pace slows. "Maybe I should do this another time. After all, we're supposed to be on a coffee date today."

"Trouble, we'll have a coffee date another day."

"You certain? You're a busy man. Maybe today is the only day you have time for a coffee date."

He chuckles.

"Wait. It's me who's busy. I don't have time for a coffee date unless we do it today."

He shrugs. "Then, we'll have a date when you do have time."

My lips purse. "You're too happy to get rid of me."

"Stop stalling."

His lips meet mine in a hard kiss. Before I have a chance to wrap myself around him, it ends. While I'm still dazed, he opens the door to the bakery and shoves me inside before shutting the door behind me.

Go he mouths as he points to Cassandra.

Some emotional support police officer he is.

Chapter 17

Forgiveness — doesn't mean anything if you don't have to grovel for it

❧

I INHALE A CLEANSING breath as I repeat my mantra to myself. *I am conquering my fears.*

The bell above the door chimes and I open my eyes to discover Peace entering the bakery behind me. He points at Cassandra.

Dude, I know who my sister is. No reason to point.

A man presses two cups of coffee into my hands.

"I didn't order these."

He pats me on the shoulder before urging me toward Cassie. What is this? Does the whole town know about my feud with my sister? What am I thinking? This is Winter Falls. They probably do.

I set one of the coffees down in front of Cassandra. She glares at me as she removes her headphones.

"What do you want?"

"To talk."

She snorts. "To talk? Yeah, right. You need something. This will go a lot quicker if you cut to the chase and tell me what you need."

I frown. Do I ignore Cassie unless I need something? I dredge up *Past Olivia's* memories and search for the last time we hung out. Crap. It's been years.

She drums her fingers on the table. "What could it be? You obviously don't need bail money. I bet dating a cop is handy."

I slam my coffee down before leaning close to get in her face. "You can be as mean and bitchy to me as you want, but you will not say anything negative about Peace. You hear me?"

Her eyes widen. "You're serious?"

A chair scrapes against the floor as Peace settles at the table next to us. He winks at me. "I am quite charming."

I roll my eyes at him before settling into a seat at the table with Cassie. "I'm serious."

"Huh. I thought you were dating a cop because you're planning a bank heist and wanted an inside man."

I giggle. "A bank heist? In Winter Falls where there are no banks?"

"There may be a flaw in my thinking."

"Ya think?"

She smiles as she lifts her coffee. "Thanks for the coffee."

"I didn't buy it. Some guy handed it to me. I'll put some money in the tip jar before I leave."

"You will?"

I sigh. Guess it's time for the whole apology explanation groveling thing. *I am conquering my fears.*

"I'm sorry."

She perks up. "Sorry for what?"

She isn't going to make this easy.

"For ghosting you."

She contemplates her coffee for several minutes as she considers my words. I try not to squirm in my seat. My gaze catches on Peace and he gives me a thumbs up. *You got this* he mouths.

I wish I could believe him.

"Why did you ghost me?"

Crap. I thought this conversation was uncomfortable before. It's about to get way more uncomfortable. I don't want to admit to any of this to anyone. Let alone to Cassandra in a public place where I know everyone's listening to me.

"Don't worry, girl. We're not listening," the man who gave me the coffees hollers from behind the cash register.

"How did you know to reassure me if you weren't listening?"

"Because your face looks like you're constipated."

I feel my cheeks heat. "C–c–constipated?"

Cassie bursts out laughing. "She always looks constipated when she has to do something she doesn't want to."

"I do not."

"Do too!"

"Do not!"

"Welp! If I didn't already know you're sisters and your resemblance to each other didn't clue me in, I'd know you grew up together now." I narrow my eyes and shoot lasers at the man behind the counter. He waves. "I'm Bryan by the way."

I swallow down my snarky reply. "Thank you for the coffees."

"Two coffees is nothing to pay for having the scoop on the gossip."

The door behind him swings open and Rowan strolls out. "Are you giving away coffee again?"

"I'll pay for it."

"I got this," Peace stands and strolls to the counter to pay for the coffees and order me an apple turnover.

Bryan looks Peace up and down. "I understand why the gossip gals chose you next. Can I touch your chest?"

Rowan grunts. "Don't let him."

"There's no need to be jealous. I'll always find your muscles the best," Bryan says to Rowan before concentrating on Peace. He bites his lower lip as his eyes roam over him.

Peace shakes his finger at him. "Nuh-uh. Don't try to flirt with me. I know who you have your eye on."

"Who does he have his eye on?"

Bryan slaps Rowan. "Never you mind."

"Bryan is my kind of person," I tell Cassie.

She rolls her eyes. "Of course, he is. He's crazy."

I wag my finger at her. "Nuh-uh. I'm not the crazy one. You are. If we're calling each other names, then I'm the snarky troublemaker."

"You got that right."

Crap. I'm not a troublemaker. Not any longer.

"I'm a reformed troublemaker."

"Am I supposed to believe this crap?"

She starts to pack up her things to leave. Double crap. This is not how I hoped my apology would go. I'm not surprised, though.

Peace arrives and places two apple turnovers on the table. "Enjoy, ladies." He pretends to tip his hat before retreating to the counter where he holds a whispered conversation with Bryan.

I dig into my treat. I'm not stalling. Much. I chew my bite as I consider how to begin. At the start, I guess.

"I felt like Mom and Dad abandoned us when they died."

Cassie pauses with the apple turnover halfway to her mouth. She clears her throat before setting it down. "Explain."

I shrug. I can't explain. It makes no sense.

"I was fifteen when they died. I needed my mom and suddenly she wasn't there."

"It's not your fault they died."

I roll my eyes. "I know. I'm not feeling guilty for a truck driver hitting their car."

"Elizabeth told you?"

Yep. Elizabeth told me all about how Cassandra convinced herself it was her fault our parents died. There's a reason I refer to Cassie as the crazy one.

I squeeze her hand. "How could you ever believe it was your fault they died? And why didn't you ever say anything?"

"Duh. Because I was wallowing in guilt."

"And you nearly ruined your relationship with Cedar because of it."

She withdraws her hand. "Nope. We're not hashing out all my problems today."

"As long as you understand it wasn't your fault, I can agree."

She crosses her arms over her chest. "The same way you agree Mom and Dad didn't abandon us on purpose?"

I walked right into that, didn't I?

"I went to see a counselor," I admit. "We worked on my feelings of abandonment for years."

"Years? When did you start going to a counselor?"

"After the last time you had to bail me out of jail. You screamed at me outside of the police station and claimed you were done with me."

She swears under her breath before reaching for my hand. "I'm sorry. I was trying the tough love thing."

"It worked. I found a counselor and I learned how to deal with my feelings about Mom and Dad dying."

"Good for you." She squeezes my hand before letting me go. "You could have discussed this with me."

"Really? You don't discuss their deaths any more than I do."

She blows out a puff of air. "True."

"Anyway." I swallow the lump in my throat. This is where it gets difficult. "When all of you left Saint Louis, those old feelings of abandonment reared their ugly heads again and I kind of went out of control."

"What happened?"

I stare out the window. I can't meet her eyes and admit what an idiot I was. "I went back to pushing my boundaries and getting into trouble."

There's no need to discuss the particulars. Cassie's bailed me out of jail often enough. She can form a picture on her own without any details on my part.

"You said you're a reformed troublemaker."

I meet her gaze so she can see the sincerity in my eyes. "I am."

"How did you get from going off the rails to becoming a reformed troublemaker?"

How I wish Cassie could be similar to Gabrielle and Elizabeth who didn't hesitate to welcome me back into the family. But no. She wants all the dirty details.

"I woke up one morning and I didn't recognize the man next to me." It wasn't the first time this happened, but Cassie doesn't need to know more than this. "And then when I went to pay for my coffee at the café my card was denied. Someone had stolen all of my money."

"What did you do?"

My cheeks darken. I'm a little ashamed of what I did next. "I begged Beckett for an advance on my trust fund, went back to a counselor, and got my shit together."

"Okay. I understand all of that. What I don't understand is why you ghosted me? I," she exclaims as she pounds her chest, "should have been the one you reached out to when you needed money. Not Beckett. I would have been on a plane to Saint Louis within an hour."

"I know. And I can't tell you how much I appreciate what you have done for me in the past. But this time I needed to do this for myself. I needed to be the person to help myself. Otherwise, how was I going to learn better?"

She chews on her lip as she considers me. "I hate when you make a good point."

"Back atcha."

We sit in silence while she mulls over everything I told her.

"Why didn't you phone me when you got your shit togeth-er?"

"Because I came here instead."

She winces. "And I treated you to bitch Cassie treatment."

I shrug. "I think the one thing we can agree on is that I deserved it."

"No one deserves bitch Cassie treatment. Except maybe Cedar when he lied about who he was."

"Cedar lied about who he was?" I plant my elbows on the table. "Tell me more."

To my relief, she launches into the entire Cedar Cassandra love story. Letting me in is her way of telling me she forgives me.

Peace snaps his fingers and catches my eye. *You good?* I nod. He mimes calling me, and I blow him a kiss.

Me? Olivia Lucy Dempsey just blew a kiss at a police officer. It's about as farfetched as Cassie falling in love with a drifter. Maybe Winter Falls is magical in addition to quirky.

Chapter 18

Surprise – should be used with caution as it may lead to tears and heartfelt confessions

✤

"WHAT IS EVERYONE DOING here?" I ask when I open the door to Beckett's house to find Elizabeth and River, Cassandra and Cedar, and Gabrielle and Phoenix standing on the stoop waiting for me.

Cassie rolls her eyes. "Duh. Helping you move."

"I brought the brawn." River flexes his biceps and strikes a pose.

Elizabeth strokes his muscles. "Good job, Casanova."

"There's no need for all of your help. I don't have any furniture yet. And I can handle some boxes on my own."

Beckett comes up behind me. "Let's go. The boxes upstairs in Olivia's room can go in Phoenix's truck. River and Cedar, you're with me."

Everyone jumps to follow his orders. I watch with my mouth gaping open. "Since when does everyone do what Beckett says?"

Elizabeth threads her arm through mine and draws me outside toward my car. "It's easier when we have lots to do."

"I'm telling you. We don't have lots to do. I don't have any furniture. I'm borrowing a bed from Beckett and I'll buy the rest when I have some cash saved." Which will be sometime in the next century.

My sisters ignore my protests as they bustle me to my car.

"I'm not buying everyone pizza and beer for helping me out when I don't need the help," I say once we're all settled in my car.

"Stop whining and drive," Cassie insists and I decide to just go with the flow.

"I will be glad to not have to drive the thirty minutes to Winter Falls all the time," I comment when we enter the town a half-hour later.

I continue to the apartment building a mere three-minute walk from *Earth Bliss.* "This is such a convenient place to live," I say as I exit the car.

"I can't believe we're moving you into my old apartment," Cassandra comments.

"I think you mean my old apartment," Elizabeth says.

"Nope. She means my old apartment," Gabrielle says.

Lilac pushes the door to the building open and steps outside. "I think you mean she's moving into *my* apartment."

"Huh? What are you doing here?"

"This is my apartment. I was preparing for your arrival," Lilac says.

"Is that how you found a place so quickly? I didn't tell you I got permission to take over *Earth Bliss* until yesterday."

Cassandra nudges me. "You didn't need to tell Lilac you got permission from the town council. She is the town council."

"I am not the town council," Lilac corrects. "But I am a member of the town council."

Cassie rolls her eyes. "You can't make one little misstep with this one."

We trudge up the stairs to the apartment.

"Let me show you around," Lilac offers.

It's a pretty basic place. The living room/kitchen/dining area is an open concept. Down the hallway are the bedroom and bathroom. Despite its simplicity, the place is nicer than anywhere I've lived on my own before.

"Knock! Knock!" Phoenix calls as he strolls into the apartment carrying two boxes. "Where do you want these?"

"Anywhere you want." I throw my arms out to indicate the empty apartment.

Gabrielle points to the hallway. "In the bedroom."

"I'll get the rest of the boxes," he says when he returns.

"I'll help." Gabrielle rushes after him.

"We won't see them for a while," Elizabeth comments after the door closes behind them.

I sigh. "It's two more boxes and a suitcase. I'll grab them myself. Then, everyone can get on with their day."

"Get on with their day?" Cassie's question has me stopping in my tracks. "This is our day. We're spending the day with our family."

"Um, okay. What do you want to do?"

"We're helping you move."

"Have you grown hard of hearing in your old age? I told you. There's nothing to move. Beckett is bringing over the bed Lilac said I could borrow and then we're finished."

"I think we should tell her," Lilac says.

"Tell me what?"

"And ruin the surprise?" Elizabeth shakes her. "No way."

"What surprise?"

"Never you mind," Cassie sings.

I pin Lilac with my gaze. She hates to lie, and I know from past interactions she believes an omission of the truth is the same as a lie. Maybe this situation qualifies.

Elizabeth steps in front of me to cut off my stare down with Lilac. "Don't look at her. She promised not to tell."

Lilac purses her lips. "A promise I'm now regretting."

"Don't worry. They're here," Cassie says from where she's standing looking out of the window.

I start toward her but Elizabeth blocks me. "Sorry. No peeking for you."

"It's official. The lot of you are crazy. There's something in the water in Winter Falls, isn't there? Am I going to go crazy since I'm living here now?"

Elizabeth snorts. "Because you're not crazy already?"

"A little help?" Beckett hollers from the hallway and I rush to open the door for him.

As soon as the door's open, he hurries in carrying a sofa together with River.

"This isn't my sofa," I tell him.

"Where do you want it?" River asks.

"This isn't mine," I repeat.

"Against this wall," Elizabeth suggests.

Beckett and River position the sofa before setting it down. Apparently, it's ignore Olivia day.

"Surprise!" Beckett announces.

"Um. What?"

Lilac steps forward. "Beckett bought you furniture for the entire apartment."

Beckett grunts at her.

"What?" She throws her arms in the air. "You did."

"And you promised you wouldn't tell her."

"No. I promised I wouldn't ruin the surprise. I can't ruin the surprise when the sofa is already here."

"But the sofa is only the beginning," Beckett argues. "There's also a kitchen table and chairs. A bed and dressers. And a television."

No! This is unacceptable. I grasp my brother's hand and drag him down the hallway to the bedroom while Elizabeth and Cassandra trail behind us.

"What are you doing?" I ask when my sisters stop me from shutting the door on them.

Elizabeth shrugs. "Isn't this a family meeting?"

"No. I want to speak to Beckett in private."

"Geez. There's no reason to be snarky." She whirls around and slams into Cassandra.

"Watch where you're going!" Cassie squeals.

"You're the one who followed me."

"A mistake I won't be making any time soon again."

Cassandra grabs Elizabeth by the bicep and limps out of the room. I slam the door behind them before confronting Beckett.

"You can't buy an apartment's worth of furniture for me."

"I know I can because I already did."

"Beckett!"

"Olivia!"

I huff and stomp my foot. *Past Olivia* urges me to give him hell, but I inhale a cleansing breath and repeat both of my mantras. *I am present in this moment. I am conquering my fears.*

Once I have my irritation under control, I try again.

"Beckett, you don't need to buy me furniture. I'm capable of buying my own furniture." Maybe not right this very minute. But eventually, I'll have some extra money to spend.

"I'm trying to do something nice for you because I know how busy you've been with teaching your yoga classes and making plans to acquire *Earth Bliss.*"

"And dating a cop!" Cassandra adds from the hallway.

"Does she have some kind of listening device?" I ask the door.

"I don't need a listening device. You always speak at top volume."

I ignore her and address Beckett. "Okay. I'll pay you back for the furniture."

He growls. "You are not paying me back. This is a present for you. To congratulate you on your new business."

I throw my hands in the air. "You can't buy me presents! I'm a horrible sister. I told you, you were dead to me."

He grasps my hands out of the air. "I know you didn't mean it."

"I didn't. I swear I didn't." My eyes itch and I sniff before I end up blubbering. Olivia Lucy Dempsey does not blubber.

"I know. I'm your big brother, remember? I know you. I know you were hurting. I don't know why. You girls and your thought processes would confound a rocket scientist."

The look of expectation on his face makes me feel guilty. Shit. I need to admit the truth. I blow out a breath and confess, "I felt like you were abandoning me."

"We asked you to move to Colorado with us," Elizabeth shouts through the door.

"Does everyone in this family have the hearing of a bat?" I mutter under my breath.

Beckett squeezes my hands. "I'm sorry you felt like I abandoned you. The job opportunity was too good to pass up." He pauses to study the floor.

"And?" I prod. He's not the only one who knows when a sibling is hiding something.

"And I hoped you'd come with us. Saint Louis held a lot of bad memories for you."

"A lot of good memories, too."

"Yeah." He smiles but his eyes are full of sadness.

"I miss them," I whisper.

"Mom and Dad would be proud of you."

I frown. "Not hardly."

"Don't sell yourself short. You've made mistakes but you're learning."

Knock! Knock!

"Are you two done with your heart-to-heart? We've got the bed," Cedar yells.

"You good?" Beckett asks.

"As long as you forgive me for being a supreme bitch."

He wraps his arms around me and hugs me tight. "You're not a bitch."

The door flies open.

"Group hug!" Elizabeth screeches before slamming into us.

I giggle. "Let me guess. She tripped again."

"Shut it. I can't help it the floor hates me."

Cassandra and Elizabeth wrap their arms around my back. "Happy to have you back," Cassie whispers.

I nod since there's something wrong with my throat.

It took me forever to get my act together, but I couldn't be happier to finally be back with my family.

Chapter 19

❧

I COLLAPSE ON THE sofa after kicking my family out of my apartment. Finally. They've been great helping me get organized and unpacked, but I'm exhausted and ready to veg out in front of my brand-freaking-new mega-sized television all by myself.

Knock! Knock!

"What did you forget?" I ask as I open the door. My brow wrinkles when I discover Peace in the hallway.

"You're not my family."

He chuckles. "I'm aware."

"Sorry. My family just left. I thought one of them came back because they forgot something." I open the door wide. "Come in."

He kisses my cheek before handing me a burlap bag. "I brought you something."

"You didn't need to," I make a token protest but I'm already digging in the bag. I remove a mug. "Clove's Coffee Corner. Olivia's mug."

"Everyone who lives in town has their own mug at Clove's."

"I love it!" I throw my arms around him. "Thank you."

"You're welcome, Livie."

My belly warms at his nickname for me. No one's ever given me a nickname before. Unless you count 'dickhead' or 'dumbass', which I definitely don't. And, no, I'm not revealing the stories behind those nicknames. Don't bother asking.

His arms loosen so he can look down at me. I notice his eyes are full of heat. Oh my. I want to stare into those eyes when they explode with fire while we're both naked and sweaty and tangled up in my sheets. I bite my bottom lip and he groans before stepping away.

"You're a little minx."

I ignore how cold I feel without his arms around me and waggle my eyebrows. "I' prefer the term femme fatale."

He snorts. "I bet you do."

"Do you want a tour?"

He frowns as he scans the living room. "I thought you didn't have any furniture? If I had known you had furniture, I would have helped you move in."

I wave away his comment. "I didn't have furniture this morning. Beckett bought me a bunch of stuff as a present."

"Must be nice," he mumbles.

Crap. Am I throwing my wealth in his face? Normally, the men I hang around with can't be more excited when they find out I have a trust fund. But Peace is not the type of man I usually hang around with. He's different. And special.

"I'm sorry," I blurt out.

"Sorry about what? What happened? What did you do?"

I frown. I thought we were past the whole accusation stage of our relationship. Maybe not.

He runs a hand through his hair. "Sorry. I didn't mean to accuse you of any wrongdoing. It's the risk of dating a police officer."

Hmm… Maybe I need to re-think this dating a cop thing. Olivia and a cop? It still sounds unbelievable.

Peace palms my neck and lays his forehead against mine. "I'll try to do better."

He's going to try to do better? I'm the one who's a mess and in need of some betterment. Not him. No siree bob. Peace is perfect. He smells yummy, looks good enough to eat, and is kind to boot.

Oh no. Oh no. Oh no. Oh no. I'm falling for Peace. A cop.

Past Olivia raises her head to sneer at me. I push her back down into the dark hole where she belongs. She needs to stay in the past. Thus, the name *Past Olivia.*

Peace squeezes my neck. "Livie? You hear me?"

I clear my throat and return my attention to the man in front of me. "We're all works in progress."

He smiles and his dimples make an appearance. Who knew dimples were irresistible on a man? Not me.

"Knock! Knock!" A voice hollers from the hallway.

I moan and tuck my head into Peace's shoulder. "Please tell me I'm hearing things."

His body shakes with his laughter. "Nope."

"The gossip gals are outside my door?"

"Yep."

He shifts us until he can open the door. "Hello, ladies."

"I knew it!" Cayenne squeals. "I knew Peace and Olivia would make a wonderful couple. Look at them. They're perfect together."

"I said it first," Feather declares. "I'm the one who reminded all of you of the appeal of an opposite."

"You are both wrong," Sage declares. "I'm the one who knew Olivia was the one for Peace. I knew the moment he returned to the station after the traffic stop when they first met."

I glance up at Peace. "What happened at the station?"

"Nothing."

Sage bustles inside with the rest of the gossip gals following her. "Nothing? Hardly. He was clearly agitated."

"He wasn't the only one," I mutter under my breath but Peace must hear me as he pinches my side.

"Behave."

I flutter my eyelashes at him. "Have you not met me?"

He clears his throat. "To what do we owe the pleasure of your company today, ladies?"

Petal lifts the basket she's carrying. "We're the welcome wagon."

She hands me the basket and I glance down to find it's full of candles. "Um, thanks for the candles?"

"Your sister didn't want any candles," she complains.

"Cassandra's afraid of fire."

"She is? Why? What happened?"

I snort. Petal can't seriously believe I'm buying her innocent act. If she wants to find out why Cassie's afraid of fire, she'll have to ask her. Because I'm not telling.

I set the basket on the kitchen table. "What else is in here?"

"There better not be a list of possible matches," Peace grumbles.

"Why not?" I ask and he scowls. "Matches are handy for the candles."

"Not, matches as in light fire but matches as in possible partners for you."

"Why would there be a list of possible partners in a welcome basket?"

"Because their welcome baskets usually include them."

"How do you know?"

His cheeks darken and he concentrates on the floor.

"Peace?"

"Because I was on the list of possible partners for Elizabeth."

I gulp. I'd forgotten all about Elizabeth and Peace dating. Does he still have feelings for her? Is he using me to get closer to her? My stomach sours. I think I'm going to be sick.

He cups my face. "Livie. Don't be upset."

What? Am I not supposed to be upset the man I'm dating dated my sister? This is a classic moment to unleash the Kraken and lose my mind.

We keep the Kraken on a leash now, New and Improved Olivia reminds me. Sometimes I want to throttle her. Seriously. Wrap my hands around her neck and squeeze until her head pops off in a gush of blood. *Past Olivia* rubs her hands together in anticipation. She's a bit bloodthirsty.

"Elizabeth and I went out on one date. One single date. She was already in love with River by then."

"I don't care how she felt," I hiss at him. The bitch has arrived at the show, and I have zero cares to give. "I want to know if the man I'm dating is in love with my sister."

Yep. I went there. Do not pass go. Proceed directly to worst case scenario.

His eyes sparkle and those dang dimples come out to play. "I'm not in love with your sister. How could I be in love with anyone else when the only woman I can see is you?"

Warmth spreads throughout my body at his response.

"Not a bad answer, Johnny Law. Not a bad answer."

"I told you we didn't need to put a list of possible matches into Olivia's welcome basket," Sage declares and I startle.

How could I forget they're here? And now they've witnessed insecure Olivia have a meltdown. Great. This is going to be all over Winter Falls by the morning.

"I still think we should have included a beginner BDSM kit," Feather says.

"A beginner BDSM kit? Please. I'm on at least intermediate level."

I'm kidding but fire lights in Peace's eyes. A picture of him tying my hands to my headboard while he's naked pops into my mind and I do a full body shiver. Where do I sign up to get that party started?

"I knew Olivia was the perfect person to take over my business," Cayenne says and brings me out of a fantasy of Peace teasing me while I'm restrained.

Peace leans down to whisper in my ear. "I vote we kick the gossip gals out and then spend the evening making out on the sofa."

"I second."

He kisses my forehead before stepping away from me.

"Thank you for the welcome gift, ladies," he says as he herds them toward the door.

"Is he kicking us out?" Clove snorts. "As if anyone can kick us out."

"You can stay if you want, but my toilet is overflowing and Peace offered to help me fix it."

"Toilet overflowing? Sure," Feather mutters.

Sage elbows her. "Maybe Peace is having plumbing problems. Get it?"

Peace shuts the door behind them.

"Lock it," I order him. "Cassandra warned me to always lock my doors in Winter Falls."

"No one locks their doors in Winter Falls."

"Do you want the gossip gals bursting back in here?"

"Good point."

He locks the door and prowls toward me. "Now, I believe you promised me a make out session, Ms. Troublemaker."

"You'll have to catch me first. I bet I can outrun you."

I can't. Totally worth it.

Chapter 20

The Brotherhood of the Dempsey Crew – not a real thing

❦

PEACE

"What's going on?" I ask when I open my front door to find Olivia's brother standing on my porch. "Is Olivia okay? Did something happen to her?"

Beckett growls. "Something happened to her all right." He pokes my shoulder. "You did."

I cross my arms over my chest and glare down at him.

"You should watch yourself. I'm a police officer."

"Being a cop isn't going to save you if you hurt Olivia. You should stay away from her."

He's at the wrong address if he thinks he can order me around. "You are not her keeper."

"No, I'm worse. I'm the big brother who raised her after our parents died." He pauses before launching into a speech.

"You don't get it. Olivia went off the rails when our mom and dad died. I did everything I could think of to bring her back. I was succeeding when I got the job opportunity in White Bridge. I thought she'd come with us. I thought she'd want to escape the bad memories. She didn't. This time when she went off the rails none of her family was there to help her. She's finally doing better. She doesn't need a man messing around with her."

I growl. "Messing around with her?"

"Messing with her head. Her priorities should be her business and her family. You are not part of the equation. Leave her alone or else."

"Or else what? And, keep in mind, I'm still a police officer."

"I don't give a shit if you're the Chief of Police. Stay away from my sister."

"I care if he's the Chief of Police," Lyric hollers as he saunters into my yard and onto my porch.

"What are you doing here? I don't need backup," Beckett tells him.

"I'm not here to back you up. I'm here to make sure I don't have to incarcerate one of my officers. Peace can be a bit of a hothead."

Great. Way to throw ammunition on the fire. "I'm not a hothead anymore."

"He's a hothead?" Beckett glares at me. "Yet another reason for him to keep away from my sister."

"It's Olivia's choice. She's an adult. If she doesn't want me around, she can tell me. Until then," I open my arms up wide. "I'm not going anywhere."

Beckett shakes his fist at me. "Now, you listen to me—"

"Oh goodie. We're not too late to catch the blood bath," River interrupts as he along with Phoenix and Cedar join us on my porch.

"What are you doing here?" I ask them.

"No idea," Cedar answers. "This is my first time."

"Lucky you." Phoenix grunts.

River winks. "We're the welcome to the brotherhood of the Dempsey crew."

Of course. I should have realized. Each one of them is with a Dempsey sister.

"The brotherhood of the Dempsey crew?" Phoenix snorts. "You can't keep it simple?"

"Simple's boring."

"Nothing wrong with boring," Cedar says.

Since they're talking nonsense, I return my attention to the man threatening me. "I don't get where all this aggression is coming from all of a sudden. You know I've been dating Olivia for a while now. You even saw us together at movie night. What changed?" I ask Beckett.

"I thought Olivia would do her thing."

"Do her thing?"

"Get rid of you as soon as the two of you…" His cheeks darken. "You know."

"You know?" River chuckles. "How old are you? Can you not say the word sex? It's not hard. Oh wait. It should definitely be hard."

Beckett shoves him. "What do you know? You don't have sisters. I raised those girls from the time our parents died. They're not merely sisters to me. They're my girls. The only family I have."

Lyric bumps his shoulder. "Not anymore. We're all family now."

"Being related to someone via marriage is not the same thing and you know it."

I decide to throw Beckett a bone before Lyric gives him a lecture about what family means. Because being related by marriage is most definitely considered family in Winter Falls. "Olivia and I are taking things slow."

"Slow? We are discussing Olivia here? My oldest sister? The one who figured out how to hotwire my truck when she was fifteen?"

I frown. I knew Olivia was a troublemaker, but hotwire a truck? That's criminal territory. "Olivia can hotwire a truck?"

"Not the point."

"I think it is the point."

Lyric shoves in between us. "Knock it off, Peace. You're not just stepping into the trap he set for you, but you're jumping feet first into it."

Fuck. He's right. Olivia's past is immaterial. She's not a criminal and she's trying to do better. Those are the important things. Not how much of a troublemaker she was as a teenager. I promised her I wouldn't judge her on her past and I intend to keep my promise.

"I was promised pancakes. When does the pancake portion of the morning begin?" Cedar asks.

"I'm with you." Phoenix checks his watch. "The diner's open."

They stroll off together in the direction of Main Street.

"How can you leave? No blood has been shed yet," River yells after them.

"And there will be no blood shed today," Lyric announces. Beckett snarls at him. "Sorry, brother, I can't allow one of my officers of the peace to get into a fight. The rest of the town will think I've lost control of my troops."

"No, we won't!" Ashlyn declares.

"I thought we were going for pancakes, dream girl."

Ashlyn rolls her eyes at her husband. "Don't tell me you believed that story. You own a bakery. Why would I want to go out for pancakes?"

Rowan plucks their baby girl out of Ashlyn's arms. "You're not getting in the middle of a fight with our daughter."

She motions toward us. "I'm not getting into a fight at all, because there is no fight. I expected more of Peace."

"You make me sound bloodthirsty."

"Because you are." She grins. "Don't you remember the time you slammed what's his name's face into a locker because he was flirting with your girlfriend?"

River raises his hand. "I'm what's his name. And I wasn't flirting with his girlfriend."

"You asked her to prom," I remind him.

"I was testing her loyalty to you. You're welcome."

"Can we get back to the matter at hand?" Beckett asks the crowd.

"What's the matter at hand?" Cassie asks as she arrives.

I don't bother asking how everyone knew to show up here this morning. This is Winter Falls after all. The second any excitement occurs everyone appears as if by magic.

"Beckett challenged Peace to a duel," Ashlyn answers.

"Do they get to pick their weapons?"

"Yes, according to the rules of dueling the challenged man has the right to choose the weapons."

Cassie giggles. "You've been narrating historical romance again, haven't you?"

"If it weren't for those uncomfortable outfits, I'd totally build a time machine and travel back to the regency period." Ashlyn fans her face. "Regency men are h-a-w-t. Hawt."

Rowan grunts. "What about me? You going to leave me behind?"

She pats his arm. "You can come with me. I bet a threesome with a regency noble would be out of this world."

"Enough," he announces before dragging her away.

"Have fun!" Cassie shouts after them.

Ashlyn gives her two thumbs up. "Don't contact me anytime today."

Cassie scans the crowd. "Where's Cedar?"

"He went to have pancakes at the diner with Phoenix," River says.

"Pancakes. Awesome." She points to Beckett. "Don't be too hard on Peace."

"You're going to leave me here with your big brother?" I call after her.

"If you're the man for Olivia, you can take care of yourself."

"I'm going to interpret your leaving as a sign of approval."

She spins around. "I'm not the one you need to worry about gaining approval from."

Beckett nods. "She's right."

"I'm not referring to you, you dweeb. Olivia's the only one he needs approval from. If she approves of him, the rest of us will fall in line." She narrows her eyes on me. "As long as you make her happy."

"I can make her happy." I smirk.

Beckett pokes me. "Are you trying to irritate me?"

"What happens if I say yes?"

"I kick your ass."

"Don't worry about him kicking your ass," River says. "He claimed he was going to kick all of our asses. Never happened."

"Do I appear worried?"

"No, but you can't expect me to pass up a chance to remind Beckett he couldn't kick my ass."

I can't argue with him there. Beckett is always fun to wind up. Take now, for instance, his face is red and a vein is pulsing in his neck. I bet I can get a muscle to tick in his jaw.

"You can't bully me into leaving Olivia alone."

A muscle ticks in his jaw. Too easy.

"If you care about her, you'd stay away."

I get in his face. "Don't you dare throw the term 'care' around. You don't know the first thing about me. And I'm beginning to think you don't know your sister very well either. She'd lose her ever loving mind if she knew you were here."

"I'm not stupid. She doesn't know I'm here."

"I don't?" Olivia asks as she pushes her way between us.

"Olivia," Beckett grumbles.

She holds up her hand. "Nope. You don't speak to me." She scans my body. "He didn't hurt you, did he?"

My heart warms at her concern for me. "I'm good."

"Great. My job here is done." She turns to leave.

I catch her hand. "Are you okay?"

She sighs. "Yeah, but I can't stay. I'm too mad."

I kiss her forehead. "Okay. I'll phone you later."

She pokes at Beckett. "You better leave here with me or I'm phoning Lilac."

He swears under his breath. "You wouldn't?" She cocks an eyebrow. "Fine. I'm leaving."

She marches away and her brother rushes after her. I chuckle as he beseeches her. She won't be forgiving him anytime soon. She'll make him grovel a bit first.

Although, she didn't make me grovel much. Despite what an ass I was when we first met. I should have never judged her based on the few pieces of paper of her criminal record. I'm past those judgments now, though.

Chapter 21

Pounding on the door — a surefire way to stop any closet shenanigans

🍀

"YOU LOOK GORGEOUS," LILAC declares when she catches me staring at myself in the mirror.

"I'm sorry. I know it's bad manners to outshine the bride," I tease.

It's the day of her wedding to Beckett and all of the bridesmaids and the bride are preparing in the bridal suite. The venue is amazing. It's a ranch on several hundred acres nestled in the foothills of the Rocky mountains. The ceremony will be held in an old barn.

I've never dreamed of a big wedding but if I had, it would've been like this. I scan the room. Except for the whole eight bridesmaids thing. For some reason, Lilac thought having all of her sisters as well as all of us Dempsey daughters as her bridesmaids was a good idea. I think she's crazy.

She frowns. "Outshine the bride?"

Cassandra rolls her eyes from behind Lilac. "Lilac doesn't understand idioms. Or teasing."

"I understand teasing and idioms. I was confused because there's no possible way she can outshine me. I'm wearing a wedding dress. All eyes will be on me."

"Lilac is joking." Ashlyn clutches her chest. "Our little Lilac has grown up."

"Those are my shoes!" Juniper yells at Ellery before nabbing the shoes she's holding.

"No, yours are over there." Ellery points to a pair of sky high heels. "You wanted to impress Maverick."

Juniper snorts. "Maverick isn't impressed by women who wear high heels."

Lilac marches to them while digging her phone out of a pocket. "I have everyone's shoe orders here."

"Who allowed her to have a dress with a pocket for her phone?" Juniper asks the room.

"It's quite handy. I had the seamstress add it." Lilac shows off the secret pocket area.

"No!" Aspen's screech cuts off any further discussion of Lilac's pocket situation. She waves toward her chest. "I'm leaking."

"You should have fed Sterling before you got dressed," her mom tells her.

"I tried. He wasn't hungry."

Ashlyn snorts. "I told you to pump."

Lilac rushes to Aspen. "This is why I suggested you choose a light-colored bridesmaid dress."

Lilac picked out the style of the bridesmaid dresses but allowed each of us to choose the color of our dress. I went for deep red.

"I'm sorry, Lilac. I'm ruining your wedding." Aspen's bottom lip wobbles.

Lilac pinches her chin. "Don't you dare cry. The make-up artist already left."

"But my dress," Aspen wails.

"Is not a problem. I was concerned this would happen and bought an extra dress for you."

Aspen's face switches from the verge of a meltdown to pissed right the eff off in a flash. "You thought I would have a boob-leakage emergency?"

"Mom! Can you handle her? I'll fetch the dress." Lilac checks her watch. "We have five minutes."

Everyone jumps to help Aspen switch dresses. I'm zipping her up when someone knocks on the door. "It's time."

We walk out of the suite and down to the main area of the barn where the ceremony will occur. Once we're lined up in front of the closed door, the groomsmen arrive.

My jaw drops to the floor when I spot Peace strutting toward me wearing a tuxedo. Holy penguins in the Antarctic! I thought he was sexy in his police uniform. I had no idea. A tuxedo has his uniform beat by about three gazillion times. He appears dashing and confident as he swaggers my way.

"What are you doing?" I manage to untie my tongue enough to ask.

He waggles his eyebrows. "Escorting you down the aisle."

Me down the aisle? Are we getting married? Whoa, Olivia! Hold your horses. You barely know this man. He's not marrying you. He's a groomsman, not the groom. My face heats with embarrassment at my wayward thoughts.

"You didn't tell me you're a groomsman," I accuse before I do something beyond stupid such as drag him down the aisle to the officiant.

He leans close to whisper. "I was sworn to secrecy."

"I guess this explains why we didn't have a rehearsal last night."

"We didn't have a rehearsal because I trust everyone here knows how to walk down an aisle," Lilac explains.

"Plus, she didn't want to pay for an extra night at the lodge," Cassandra adds.

"Beckett would have paid." Money isn't an issue for my brother. Unlike myself, he invested the money we inherited from our parents well and could live on the dividends for the rest of his life.

Ellery groans. "Don't start. I can't listen to another argument about who is responsible for paying for a wedding again."

The music changes to indicate it's time for the ceremony to begin. Peace offers me his arm.

"I hope we're not walking behind Elizabeth. Collateral damage is real."

Elizabeth glares at me. "When are you going to stop insinuating I'm a klutz?"

I shrug and she whirls around to find her place and promptly barges into Cassandra. Cassie grabs Cedar to steady herself before she falls but knocks him off balance in the process and the two tumble to the floor on top of Elizabeth and River.

The doors open on cue and everyone in the barn glances back to discover four of the wedding party in a heap on the ground.

"Are they having an orgy?" Petal asks. "Someone take pictures."

The wedding photographer is already snapping away. I have a feeling these pictures are going to be my favorite from today.

"I've always wanted to have an orgy at a wedding," River comments as he gets to his feet. He offers a hand to Elizabeth who snarls at him.

"We are not having an orgy."

"A foursome?"

"Is your sister always such a klutz?" Peace whispers.

"Yep," I answer at the same time Elizabeth exclaims, "I'm not a klutz."

Lilac sighs before marching forward to line everyone up again.

"You can't complain," Ashlyn tells her. "You're the one who thought it would be a good idea to have eight bridesmaids."

Mrs. West shoves Lilac behind her. "You can't be seen before it's your turn to walk down the aisle."

Lilac rolls her eyes. "All of a sudden you're Mrs. Traditionalist? If it were up to you, I'd be getting married in a pagan ceremony in Winter Falls."

Mr. West grasps Lilac by the shoulders and escorts her to the end of the line. "Let your mother handle this."

"Aren't weddings supposed to be boring?" I ask Peace.

"Not in Winter Falls."

The music starts up again and, as we're the first couple, we begin our march down the aisle.

"We're first. Does this mean we're the black sheep of the family?" I ask Peace.

He winks at me. "You know it."

I smile and my gaze catches Beckett's. He's frowning at us. I resist the urge to stick my tongue out at him. When we reach the altar, I break with tradition – no one could ever accuse me of being a traditionalist – and approach Beckett.

"I'm happy for you, Beckett boy. Lilac's perfect for you." I kiss him on the underside of his chin before making my way to my spot at the end of the row.

It takes a while for everyone from the wedding party to enter – eight bridesmaids is a bit over the top – but once everyone's in place, the ceremony itself doesn't last long. My feet aren't even starting to ache when Peace grasps my hand and drags me down the aisle.

"Is this some kind of race?" I giggle.

He doesn't answer as we rush past the receiving line down the hallway.

"Where are we going?"

He tries a door. When it opens, he herds me inside.

I scan the room and laugh when I realize we're in a broom closet. "What are you up to?"

He palms my neck and yanks until my body crashes into his. "You've been torturing me for the past hour. That dress. Those heels. The red lipstick on your luscious lips. I'm ready to dirty you all up."

I shiver. I one-hundred percent approve of this plan.

"What are you waiting for?"

"Your agreement."

My agreement, huh? With these heels on, my mouth is nearly at the same height as his. How fortuitous.

"How's this for agreement?" I ask and nip his bottom lip.

He groans before cradling my face in his hands and crushing his lips to mine. I thread my hands through his hair as he devours my mouth. I'm not one to be a passive participant in a kiss, though. My tongue searches for his and we duel for supremacy.

He punches his hips and his hard length hits my center. Oh my. I'm wearing heels more often if it means our bodies align up in such a glorious manner. I attempt to lift my leg to wrap it around his waist, but my dress is too tight. I grunt. Peace doesn't pause with devouring my mouth and reaches down to scrunch up my skirt until my leg is free.

Bang! Bang! Bang!

I wrench my lips from Peace to shout, "Stop banging on the door!"

"You're the one who needs to stop banging!" Elizabeth shouts back.

Peace groans and drops his forehead against my shoulder. I pat his back.

"We'll continue this later."

His head whips up and he smirks. "Later?"

"Yep. In bed."

I'm done with taking things slow. Having sex with the man I'm dating will not make me regress into *Past Olivia. Past Olivia* never dated. Her commenting privileges about my sex life with a man I'm dating are hereby revoked.

Besides, I think I'll explode if this man doesn't provide me with some satisfaction soon.

"Later." His word sounds like a promise. And it's a promise I plan to cash in on.

Chapter 22

❧

PEACE

It's impossible to pay any attention to the wedding reception with my mind constantly conjuring up images of Olivia with her lips swollen from my kisses. Olivia with her hair mussed from my hands running through it. Olivia naked in my bed.

The little minx tempts me throughout dinner. She moans as she chews her food with her eyes closed. She licks her fork before sucking on it. And when I growl at her for teasing me, she bites her bottom lip while batting her eyelashes.

She's gone too far now. I sneak my hand down her leg until I find the hem of her dress. Her eyes widen as I bunch up the material until I can touch her smooth skin. I draw lazy circles on the area behind her knee until she squirms in her seat.

Time to move on. I draw my hand up her thigh until I reach the edge of her panties. Her breath hitches and my hand retreats down her leg to her knee. Two can play at this teasing game.

I resume drawing lazy circles in her skin until she grabs my hand and tries to force it higher. I shackle her wrist and shake my head at her. She glares at me but I hold her gaze until she releases my hand.

I tease her for a few more minutes before gliding my fingers once again up her silky smooth thigh. This time when I reach the edge of her panties, she lets her legs fall open.

I lean close to whisper in her ear. "Are your panties wet for me?"

Her cheeks darken as she nods.

"I need to hear your answer."

"Yes," she hisses.

"Shall I check?"

"P-p-please."

I smirk at the stutter in her voice. Glad to hear she's effected by me as much as I am by her.

I skim my finger along the edge of her panties. Back and forth. Back and forth. Getting closer and closer to her center but always retreating just before I reach the area she's desperate for me to touch. She scooches closer to me in her seat and I freeze.

"I'm in charge," I growl at her.

She narrows her eyes at me. She prefers to be in charge, but if she wants me to give her what she needs, she'll have to relinquish control to me. Her eyes close and she inhales a deep breath. When her eyes open again, the resolve is clear.

"Good girl," I whisper and reward her with a swipe of my finger up and down the crotch of her panties. As I suspected, they're soaked. Damn, this girl is responsive to me.

She bites her lip to hold back her moan.

A microphone screeches before Lyric speaks. "It's the moment you've all been waiting for. The best man's speech."

Oh, this is perfect. I can torture Olivia while he talks and she can't say a thing.

"I haven't known Beckett long…"

I pull Olivia's panties to the side and draw a finger up and down her outer lips. She tries opening her legs again, but I clamp my hand down on her thigh.

Her eyes throw daggers at me. I grin in response and her nostrils flare.

"I couldn't imagine the type of man who would marry Lilac, a woman I've known my entire life, but Beckett is …"

As Lyric continues his speech, Olivia focuses her attention on him, although I know it's a pretense since all of her attention is focused on what my hand is doing to her body.

I reward her by spreading her outer lips and glancing my finger over her clit. She gasps.

Applause erupts. Lyric's best man speech must be finished. I didn't hear a word of it and I couldn't care less.

I straighten her panties, fix the skirt of her dress, and stand.

"Let's go," I demand as I offer her my hand.

She takes my hand but frowns when the music starts up. "We can't. We have to dance together."

I bend over until I can whisper in her ear. "I'm planning on a whole lot of dancing together of the horizontal variety."

I watch as goosebumps travel over her skin. I bite her earlobe and she shivers. I love how responsive she is to me. I can't wait to test how receptive she is once we're alone in my room with a bed.

Lilac and Beckett walk to the dance floor as the band plays *You Make It Easy*.

Cassandra laughs. "Did you ever think Beckett would dance to a country song at his wedding?" she asks Olivia.

"Um…"

"You okay? You're a bit flushed." Cassie frowns. "How much have you had to drink?"

Pain flashes across Olivia's face at Cassie's accusation. This is my fault. I should accept the blame, but I know how important it is for Olivia to repair her relationship with Cassie and clamp my mouth shut.

Olivia does an exaggerated eye roll. "Do you honestly believe Beckett had any influence over anything in this wedding? This is Lilac's show."

Cassie studies her sister for a moment before agreeing. "True. We know who wears the pants in their family."

"Would the rest of the bridal party please join the bride and groom on the dance floor?" the DJ announces and I scowl. I'm ready to throw Olivia over my shoulder and haul her out of this barn like a caveman.

Olivia bounces out of her chair with a smile stretched from ear to ear on her face. "Time to dance, Johnny Law."

"Let's go, trouble."

I lead her to the dance floor and pull her into my arms. She gasps when she feels my hard length against her.

"Can you dance with that rod in your pants?"

I chuckle as the music changes and *I Won't Give Up* begins to play.

Olivia's eyes widen when she realizes what song is playing and she seeks out Beckett who points to her. "Not giving up on you, Olivia. Never ever."

She bites her lip as she nods in response.

"Me either," Cassie yells from her side of the dance floor.

Olivia's eyes swell as she sniffs. I tighten my hold on her as I sway her back and forth to the music.

"Don't cry, honey," I beseech. "I got you."

She buries her head in my shoulder. "I'm not crying. You're crying."

I grin as I grasp her hand and spin her. She giggles as she twirls around.

"Johnny Law can dance?"

"My mom wanted a girl and Cayenne used to teach dance lessons."

"Please tell me you took ballet classes and wore a pink tutu."

"Boys don't wear tutus. They wear tights."

"You did do ballet," she squeals.

I can't resist her happiness. "And jazz and ballroom dancing."

"There's more to you than meets the eye, JL."

"Right back atcha, trouble." I wink.

The music changes to *We Are Family*. Cassie screams before rushing toward us and hauling Olivia away to the middle of the dance floor where Elizabeth and Gabrielle await them.

The sisters make a circle and sing the lyrics as they wave their arms around in what I assume is some type of dance. Ashlyn crashes through their circle.

"I'm family, too, now," she declares as she dances in the middle of the circle.

"We are, too," Juniper adds from the other side of the dance floor where she's helping Ellery and Aspen drag Lilac across the floor.

"This is my day. You're not supposed to push me around on my wedding day," Lilac complains.

"This is a family activity."

At Aspen's declaration, Lilac sighs before marching across the floor to where Olivia and her sisters are. Juniper joins Ashlyn in the middle of the circle and they dance together while the rest of the women clap and cheer them on.

Olivia catches my eye and waves before blowing me a kiss. I shake my head at her antics. This is not how I expected her to act at a wedding, but I'm happy she's happy. I'd do anything to make her happy.

I pause at the thought. *I'd do anything to make Olivia happy?* What the hell? Am I falling for her? I am. I am falling for her. The realization rocks me but before I have a chance to catch my breath, Beckett joins me on the edge of the dance floor and clasps a hand on my shoulder.

"She's happy." His hand tightens on my shoulder. "You better not hurt her."

I sigh. Are we back to this again?

"I won't."

"Good. We understand each other."

I can't resist poking him. "Does this mean you'll stop threatening to beat me up?"

"Never."

"So much for understanding each other," I grumble.

"Don't fuck this up," he orders before walking away.

The music switches to *Uptown Funk* and Olivia screams, "This is my jam!"

She rushes across the dance floor to me and grasps my hands. "Dance with me," she insists as she tugs me toward the dance floor

I resist. "Maybe I don't like this song."

She gasps and releases my hands to clutch her chest. "Tell me you're joking. Right this minute!"

I chuckle. "Come on, dancing queen."

I lead her back to the dance floor where she begins some complicated routine. So much for my plan to get Olivia naked as soon as possible.

Chapter 23

Restraints – not necessarily handcuffs

‍

"Thank you for staying for the reception," Olivia says as she skips barefoot toward my cabin while swinging her shoes in her hand.

"Why are you thanking me?"

She throws her arms out and whirls around in circles. "Because I know you wanted to drag me by my hair back to your cave after dinner."

I throw my head back and burst into laughter. She stops whirling around to watch me.

"But you didn't. You were a gentleman."

I growl. "I wasn't much of a gentleman during dinner or have you forgotten?"

She taps her cheek. "I can't remember." She looks up at me from beneath her lashes. "Maybe you need to remind me."

This is better than yes. This is a green light.

I wind my arm around her waist and throw her over my shoulder.

"My shoes!" she shouts as they clatter to the ground.

I'm not leaving those here. I reach down to grab them.

"Hold onto those, Livie. I may need them later."

"Later? Why?"

"I've been imagining you laying on my bed while wearing nothing but those shoes for hours."

She shivers at my declaration. "I'd hate to disappoint you."

"Now we're getting somewhere."

"Where are we going?"

"To my cabin."

She gasps. "You're taking me to a cabin in the woods? I hope there aren't any monsters out here."

I laugh and indicate the lights illuminating the pathway to the cabins. "We're not exactly in a remote location."

"Darn. I can't scream in ecstasy then."

"Challenge accepted."

She slaps my back. "I was joking. I'm not a screamer."

This time I don't respond aloud but the words *Challenge accepted* reverberate through my mind. I will get this woman to scream my name in passion if it takes me all night. I hope it takes me all night.

We reach my cabin and I dig into my back pocket for the key, but it's not there. Damnit. I have plans. Urgent plans. The last thing I want to do is walk back to the barn to ask for another key.

"Looking for this?" Olivia dangles the keycard in front of my face.

"You picked my pocket?"

"I prefer to say I discovered treasure while I was researching the muscles of your buttocks."

"Buttocks?"

I chuckle as I unlock the door. Once we're inside, I lift Olivia from my shoulder. I slide her down my front making sure I can feel every inch of her body before setting her on her feet.

"Are you ready for this?"

She raises her eyebrows in challenge. "Are you ready for this?"

She doesn't wait for a response and hikes up her dress before jumping and wrapping her legs around me. I catch her and spin us around until she's pressed up against the door.

"Are you trying to kill me?"

She waggles her eyebrows. "Can orgasms kill?"

"You got jokes, do you?"

"I got all the jokes," she claims. "What did the toaster say to the slice of bread?"

"What?"

"I want you inside me. Hint. Hint. Nudge. Nudge."

There's no waiting for me to take the hint. Not with my Livie. She flattens her hands against the door and uses the leverage to rub her center against my cock. I groan. She wasn't kidding about trying to kill me.

I squeeze her waist to stop her movements. "Did you forget who's in charge here?"

"I didn't realize we'd agreed to a hierarchy. Do I have to call you sir?"

Her eyes sparkle as she teases, but I'm serious. I'm in charge.

"You may call me sir, but it's not required."

She wiggles in my hold and I use my body to flatten her against the door. She's now trapped with no room to maneuver.

"Do you understand I'm in charge now?"

She smirks before declaring, "I'm not wearing any under-wear."

My cock jumps. He's ready to accept the invitation she's obviously making.

"Where are your panties?"

"In my purse."

I growl. "I wanted to remove your panties."

She shrugs. "You were too slow."

Too slow. I'll show her too slow. I whirl her around and march to the bed. She giggles as I throw her on it.

"Yeah! My evil plan is working."

She has no idea, but I can let her believe she's winning for a while. I glide my hands up her legs; gathering the fabric of her dress as I go. When I reach the apex of her thighs, she widens her legs to display herself to me.

"See? No panties?"

I groan and force myself to ignore her pussy begging me to enter her. My cock protests, but I ignore him. I'm in charge here.

I continue bunching up the dress until I reach the underside of her breasts.

"No bra either."

I'm supposed to be the one doing the teasing here. I leave her dress where it is and bite down on her nipple through the material. Her legs move to wrap around me but I press her thighs into the mattress.

She arches her back and shoves her breasts toward me. I don't take the bait. I resume rolling up her dress and push the fabric up until she's completely naked and bared to me. I have to agree the no underwear is a time saver.

I use the material of the dress to tie her hands to the headboard.

"Oh, kinky," she says as she playfully tugs on the restraint.

I roll off the bed and strip off my shirt while toeing off my shoes. When I return to the bed with my pants on, she pouts.

"If I promise to be a good girl, will you get naked and get inside of me?"

My cock twitches and I feel pre-cum gather at the head. I need to calm down before I come in my pants like a teenager.

Olivia bats her eyelashes. "Please. Pretty please. Pretty please with sugar on top."

Crap. I can't deny her. "Next time, I'm taking my time and tasting every inch of your body."

"Hell, yeah you are. I insist."

I push off of the bed and shove my pants down my legs. My cock juts out eager to find his way inside Olivia. I wrap a hand around it and squeeze to the point of pain to gain some control.

"Yes," Olivia hisses while rubbing her legs together. "Keep going."

"I thought you wanted me in you?"

She widens her legs in invitation.

I dig a condom out of my wallet and don it before kneeling on the bed.

"You sure?"

"I'm sure, Johnny Law. I'm really fucking sure."

I groan at her use of the word fuck when I'm about to do exactly that to her.

I cover her with my body my cock poised at her opening. "Hold on tight."

I slam into her until my balls slap her skin. She moans as she winds her legs around my waist. When I stay planted, she wiggles. "Move."

"Give me a sec."

"Don't tell me you're a five-second man," she taunts.

I know she's teasing but my cock is ready to detonate in her body. He's found his home and he's not moving out. Too bad for him, I'm in charge here.

I slowly pull out before plunging back into her. "Is this what you want?"

"Yes," she sighs as her eyes close and her head falls back.

I sit on my haunches and throw her legs over my shoulders as I continue to pump into her. Her tits bounce in an invitation I can't refuse. I knead and massage her breasts and her walls tighten around me.

"Give it to me, Livie," I growl.

Her head whips up and her eyes meet mine. "Almost."

I pinch her nipples and twist.

"Yes," she shouts as her pussy clamps down on my cock and she comes.

I continue to surge into her over and over to draw out her orgasm.

"My turn," I mutter when she collapses against the bed.

I lift her legs from my shoulders and bend over her while I prop myself on my elbows. I close my eyes and allow myself to feel every ripple of her walls against my cock.

Olivia wraps her legs around my waist and twists until I'm on my back and she's looming over me. Her dress hangs from one of her wrists.

"Next time I'm bringing the handcuffs."

She winks. "Bring it on, lawman. Bring it on."

My response gets caught in my throat when she braces her hands on my chest and lifts before slamming back down on my cock. Her tits bounce, the bed shimmies, and I clench my jaw before I come.

She reaches down to cup my balls and I give up the fight.

"Fuck, Livie. I'm coming."

She continues to work herself up and down my cock as my climax tears through my body.

No wonder I'm falling for this woman. She's my match in bed. Only time will tell if she's my match outside of it as well.

Chapter 24

Sober – a prerequisite for certain bedtime activities

✤

WHISTLES ERUPT WHEN I walk into Aspen's bookstore, *Fall Into A Good Book,* for the book club a few days after Lilac's wedding. The place is packed. All the gossip gals are here. Of course. All of my sisters and the West daughters are here, too. Except for Lilac who's on her honeymoon with Beckett in an undisclosed location.

"Boom chicka woo woo," Ashlyn shouts and the rest of the room takes up the chant until I stick my fingers in my mouth and let out a loud whistle.

"Great balls of fire. Can you teach me how to whistle?" Ashlyn asks.

Juniper groans. "No. Please promise me you won't teach her. She's enough of a menace as it is."

"It's true." Ashlyn smiles. "I am a menace." She walks off shouting, "Mom! Why didn't you give me a name to rhyme with menace?"

Aspen rushes forward bouncing Sterling in her arms. "Come in. Don't let everyone frighten you off."

"We're not scaring her," Sage claims.

"Yeah, we're congratulating her on landing the most eligible bachelor in Winter Falls," Cayenne adds with a wink.

"She means boinking the most eligible bachelor," Clove explains.

The gossip gals are wearing bright pink t-shirts with the words *Gossip Gals Read Smut* on them. I should ask them where they bought them. I want one. Except without the words gossip gals on it. And maybe not in bright pink. Never mind. I'll find my own t-shirt.

I curtsey. "Thank you. It was a hard job but someone had to do it."

"How hard was it?" Sage asks. "And how long?"

I wag my finger at her. "Nuh-uh. No details for you."

"Why not?" She pouts.

I hold up *Irresistible Trouble* by Pippa Grant, aka the book we read for book club. "Didn't you get enough sex in here to satisfy you?"

Ashlyn's hand shoots in the air. I point to her. "Can you ever have enough sex to satisfy you?"

A memory of falling asleep after the second time Peace took me pops into my mind. Yep. You can definitely have enough sex to be satisfied.

I wiggle my eyebrows. "What's wrong? Is Rowan not satisfying you?"

Cassandra claps her hands over her ears. "Ugh! No. Rowan is my brother-in-law. I don't want to hear about his sexual prowess."

"Brother-in-law?" Elizabeth exclaims. "Is there something you need to tell us?"

"Yeah." I nod. "Did you elope and forget to mention it?"

Cassandra snorts. "It's only an expression. Elizabeth would kill me if I eloped."

"We should all elope," Juniper suggests in a whisper.

"What did you say?" Mrs. West stomps through the room.

"Nothing."

Mrs. West points at her. "You will not be eloping, Juniper Berry West."

"But it would be much easier. Have you ever tried to plan a wedding for a movie star? It's impossible."

Mrs. West crosses her arms over her chest. "No, I haven't because someone won't let me help her."

Juniper rolls her eyes. "I asked for suggestions and the first thing you proposed was jumping over fire instead of a broom."

"I jumped over a broom at my wedding," Aspen says.

"Maverick's agent would strangle me if we had a fire jump in our ceremony."

"Is there wine?" I whisper to Cassandra.

She frowns at me. When is she going to accept I'm not going to get drunk and race through the town square naked every time I have a drink? Although, what's the harm in a bit of streaking? Nudity isn't a crime in Winter Falls anyway.

"This is great entertainment," I power on.

Gabrielle offers me a glass of red wine. I raise it to her in salute before taking a sip.

"Who do you think would win in a mud wrestling contest?" I indicate the mother and daughter who are now arguing over wearing shoes at her wedding. "Juniper or Mrs. West?"

Mrs. West pauses in her tirade about how bad shoes are for the environment and turns to me, "Isn't it about time you start calling me Ruby? After all, you'll be staying in Winter Falls for a while, won't you?"

"Of course, she's staying. She's going to operate *Earth Bliss,*" Cayenne says.

Ruby shakes her head. "I meant because she's in love with a local boy."

"They can turn on you on a dime," Gabrielle whispers as she slips behind me.

"I'm not in love with a local boy," I claim.

I'm not. Am I falling for the guy? I think I might be. *Past Olivia* snubs her nose at me. She can't believe I'm considering loving a cop. As if I have a choice in the matter.

Ruby crosses her arms over her chest and glares at me. "You're using him for sex?"

Ellery's mouth gapes open. "What are you saying, Mom? You're the one who thinks everyone should enjoy sex and passes out condoms every chance she gets."

"Speaking of which." Ruby digs into her purse and pulls out an extra-large box of condoms. "Here. You're going to need these."

I hold up my free hand and inch backwards. Gabrielle clutches my shirt before I crash into her.

"I don't need your condoms."

Ruby shakes the box at me. "Are you using prophylactics? Peace is a nice boy, but you can't be sure he isn't carrying some type of sexually transmitted disease until he's been tested."

Nice boy? She doesn't know the first thing about him if she believes he's a 'nice boy'. There's nothing nice about Peace. At least not when he's in bed. The clean-shaven, straitlaced police officer becomes a demon when the clothes come off. Go me!

"She better be using prophylactics," Cassie declares. "Beckett will kill her if she doesn't."

I shake my finger at her. "I'm not the one who couldn't figure out how to put the condom on a banana in sex class."

Ruby rips the package open. "It's quite easy. Let me show you."

Cassie's cheeks darken as she backs away. "No thanks. I've got it."

This is getting good. "I, for one, would pay good money to watch Cassandra put a condom on a banana."

"Here!" Aspen hollers and throws me a banana.

"You just happen to have a banana laying around for such an occasion?"

"I bought it for Sterling."

Ruby frowns at her. "Sterling is entirely too young to eat a banana."

Aspen mouths *You're welcome* at Cassie before escaping to the back room with her mother chasing after her.

"I can't believe I considered not showing today," I say as I sip on my wine.

"Were you chicken?" Cassandra flaps her arms.

"I'm not a chicken."

"Are you sure? Bwak. Bwak."

Ashlyn joins Cassie and the two of them begin to run in circles around the bookstore while flapping their arms like wings.

The door bangs open and Peace struts inside.

Tingles flow through me as I scan his body and memories of how he can use that body to bring me to ecstasy flash into my mind. Too bad he's not naked right now, although the uniform he's wearing works for him big time. Those uniform pants hug his thighs just right.

"Whoo-hoo! The stripper has arrived," Sage shouts and the rest of the gossip gals cheer.

Peace ignores them and shackles my wrist before hauling me outside of the bookstore.

"Is something wrong?"

"Besides you wearing a tight sweater and painted on jeans on those long legs of yours?"

I look up at him from beneath my lashes. "You like my outfit?"

"Livie, your outfit is killing me."

I bat my eyelashes. "Do you need me to help relieve your suffering?"

He groans and runs a hand through his hair. "I have another two hours until my shift ends."

"Why don't you stop by my apartment on your way home?"

He nods to my glass of wine. "How many of those have you drunk?"

I frown. What is it with everyone being concerned about how much I drink lately?

"I'm not accusing you of having too much," he's quick to say. "But I don't know if I can carry out the things I have planned if you're inebriated."

I throw the contents of the glass over my shoulder. "Not inebriated. Not even close. This was my first glass."

He grins and his dimples come out to play. I want to dip my tongue in those crevices and taste his skin. It's strictly for research purposes. I need to confirm he tastes as good as I remember from the night of the wedding.

He nods toward the bookstore. "Will you be finished with book club by then?"

I glance behind me to discover everyone has their face pressed to the window eavesdropping on us. "Does no one in Winter Falls understand the word privacy?"

"Nope."

I can work with this.

"You want to have a threesome," I say in a loud voice.

His brow wrinkles. "A threesome?"

"Work with me here," I mutter out of the side of my mouth.

He chuckles before clearing his throating and shouting, "Yes! With two women."

I poke his chest. "No way, Peace. If we're having a threesome, it's with two men. Hard limit."

"You're a fruitcake," he whispers as he pulls me near.

"Ooh. Fruitcake. Does this mean I get to soak myself in alcohol?"

He kisses my hair. "I need to get back to work. I'll see you later."

"I'll be waiting with bells on. And no underwear."

He laughs as he walks away. I sigh. How the hell did I get this lucky? A man who matches my sexual appetite and is also kind and considerate and can be a goofball at times? Jackpot!

Chapter 25

Freak out – can be enhanced with the use of plastic wrap

🦋

THE BELL OVER THE door at *Earth Bliss* chimes and Peace struts inside.

My brow wrinkles. "What are you doing here?"

"I promised to help you get this place in tiptop shape."

I don't have the money – or, rather, I don't want to borrow the money from Beckett – to do a complete makeover on the yoga studio, but I do want to give it my own touch. New paint is the first item on the agenda. New yoga blocks and new mats will have to wait.

Peace promised to help me out on his off day, which is today. "But you worked until the middle of the night."

To my utter disappointment, he rang me after I got home from smutty book club to cancel our assignation.

"I'm okay." The yawn makes him a liar.

"Go on. Go home." I shove him toward the door.

"Is this any way to greet your man?"

"What do you prefer? For me to jump you the second you walk in the door?"

He waggles his eyebrows. "I wouldn't be opposed to the idea."

"You couldn't handle me attacking you."

"Is this a challenge?" He drops his voice. "I'm all in."

I shiver. Let's do this. A whole day in bed tangled up in the sheets with Peace? I don't vote yes. I vote hell, yeah. *Past Olivia* pulls out the pompoms and begins a cheer.

What the hell? Why is she showing up now? I glance down and notice the buckets of paint and materials on the ground. My shoulders sag. There will be no spending the day with the man I'm falling for in bed. *Past Olivia* throws the pompoms on the ground before stomping away. Good riddance to the Queen of Bad Ideas.

I clear my throat. "Anyway, you should get some rest. I can finish this on my own."

He winds an arm around my neck before hauling me to him. "Don't be silly, Livie. I'm here to help." He kisses my hair. "Use me however you want."

Before I decide to use him to relieve me of my sexual frustration, I step away. "What was the emergency last night anyway? I didn't hear any sirens."

"If you hear sirens in Winter Falls, pack your bag and go. Sirens are strictly for catastrophic events."

"Really?" I raise an eyebrow. "Last night wasn't catastrophic?"

He chuckles. "Hardly. A llama escaped the wildlife refuge last night and tore down one of Phoenix's fences and his goats got loose. I was up half the night chasing the little fuckers around."

"What about the llama? Where's he?"

"Lucy's fine. Maverick was at the refuge yesterday and didn't stop by to see her, so she decided to take matters into her own hands. Paws? Hooves? Whatever."

"Lucy is my kind of gal. She knows what she wants and doesn't hesitate to go for it."

He chuckles. "Maverick was less impressed when Lucy showed up on their patio and tried kicking in their door. Juniper's dogs went nuts and there began a barking versus clucking fight."

"I need to meet this llama. She sounds full of drama. A drama llama in the flesh."

"Juniper is always happy to show off her pets at the refuge."

I was joking but I scratch 'go to the wildlife refuge' on my mental to-do list right below 'get Peace naked and have my wicked way with him'. The wildlife refuge can wait.

Peace rubs his hands together. "Are we going to stand here all day gabbing or are we going to get to work?"

"You sure you're up to it?" He growls and I hold up my hands. "Okay. Okay. Let's get going."

I lock the door to *Earth Bliss.* Lesson learned there. And lead him to the studio. "I'm painting all the walls today."

Peace removes his jacket and rolls up his sleeves. "Let's do this."

Huh. Do what? Massage those forearms? I'm on board.

Fingers snap in front of my face. "Livie? Are you daydreaming?"

I'm dreaming all right. My mouth. His muscles. I clear my throat. "Sorry. Let's get to work."

I unfold the plastic sheeting, but instead of laying it on the floor, I cover myself with it.

I hold my arms straight out and march toward Peace. "Bring me to your leader."

"You will not destroy our planet," he says before he jumps and tackles me to the ground.

I flail my arms and legs in a vain attempt to fight him off. "I come in peace. I come in peace."

He crawls on top of me and wraps his limbs around me to incapacitate me. "I think you mean Peace comes in me."

My breath whooshes out of me. Dirty Peace has arrived at the party. Dirty Peace is my favorite. I think I'll keep him. For ever and ever.

The thought startles me and I literally jolt in Peace's arms. Holy crap. I'm in love with Peace. What the hell am I going to do? There's no way he could ever love me. He hated me not too long ago. Shit. Shit. Shit.

I'm on the verge of a major freakout and not because I'm trapped in plastic – been there, done that – when there's a knock on the door.

Peace jackknifes to his feet before helping me to stand and unwinding the plastic wrap twisted around my body. I'm too busy freaking out to help and stand there like a statue as he handles the mess I've made of the plastic.

"I'll get the door," he announces and walks away.

"Surprise!" Cassandra shouts as she charges into the studio with Elizabeth and Gabrielle on her heels.

"What are you doing here?"

"Duh. We're here to help you paint."

"How do you even know I'm painting today?"

Elizabeth giggles. "Winter Falls."

"Don't worry," Gabrielle says. "You get used to the lack of privacy after a while."

Peace sidles up next to me. "Sorry. This is my fault. I mentioned my plans to help you out today to Phoenix when I was out on the farm chasing his goats."

"Chasing his goats? What do you mean?" Cassandra asks.

"The fence was damaged yesterday and a bunch of them escaped," Gabrielle explains.

Cassandra's eyes widen and she pushes up on her tiptoes. "Escaped?" she shrieks. "There are devil goats in town?" She scans the room as if she expects a goat to jump out and attack her any second.

Elizabeth barks out a laugh while Gabrielle huffs and fists her hands on her hips.

"My goats aren't devils," Gabrielle insists.

"Are you certain? Devils are exceptional at hiding their true identity," Cassandra says.

Gabrielle throws her arms in the air. "I can't with her and the goats. I just can't."

Elizabeth smirks. "I can," she whispers before getting on all fours and crawling behind Cassandra. "Baa!"

"ARGH!" Cassie screams and races toward the rear exit of the studio. She crashes into the wall of windows and then bounces back before her legs give out and she slumps to the floor.

Elizabeth jumps to her feet and points down at Cassie. "Ha! I'm not the klutz in the family. You are!"

Cassie grabs Elizabeth's leg and yanks her down to the ground. They roll around as they slap each other.

"Klutz!"

"Scaredy-cat!"

"Clumsy!"

"Chicken!"

Peace crosses his arms over his chest as he stares down at them. "Are you two about done?"

Elizabeth freezes, but Cassie gets in one more slap before she stops.

"Now, I'm done," she declares and climbs to her feet. "But it's all her fault."

I offer Elizabeth a hand and help her to stand.

"It's not my fault you're a scaredy-cat who's afraid of goats," Cassie taunts.

"Butterfingers!" Cassie launches herself at Elizabeth who shuffles behind me.

Peace moves to stop her before Cassie can touch me in her effort to get to Elizabeth. "I said enough!"

This time Cassie freezes at his order. "You used the cop voice on me," she accuses.

"I'll use more than the cop voice on you if you harm Olivia."

Her eyes widen before a smile slowly spreads over her face. "I approve," she says and turns away. "Now, are we going to paint this morning or is everyone going to goof around?"

"You're the one who—"

I slap a hand over Elizabeth's mouth and shake my head. We're not playing the blame game today.

"What color is this?" Gabrielle asks. She already has the paint opened and is mixing it.

"Ivory."

Cassandra peeks into the paint can. "It's white."

"It's ivory," I insist.

She ignores me. "The walls are white. I don't understand why we're painting the walls the same color as they already are."

Peace clamps a hand over my shoulder before I can show my sister what the difference between white and ivory is with my fist.

"She's trying to provoke you."

Cassie beams over at me. "And it's working."

"You know who's working?" I ask the room. "No one." I clap my hands. "Come on. Between the five of us, we'll have the studio painted in no time."

And then I can drag Peace back to my lair and have my wicked way with him.

Chapter 26

Handy – being able to do a handstand

❧

Olivia giggles as she lets us inside her apartment.

"I'm a ghost." She waves her arms around. "Booooo."

She's not a ghost but she is covered in white paint.

"I've never seen grown adults have a paint fight before."

"You obviously don't have siblings."

I flinch. I've always wanted siblings, but my parents never had any other children after me. I begged them for a brother when I was a kid, but they never responded.

Olivia flings her arms around me. "I'm sorry. I'm a careless cow. I should have kept my mouth shut."

I chuckle. "And, now, I'm covered in paint."

She glares at me. "You should have been covered in paint already. Who hides in the alley when there's a paint fight?"

"A man who doesn't act like a child."

She rolls her eyes. "Sometimes letting your inner child out is the adult thing to do."

I wipe the paint from her forehead and show her my now white finger. "Even if you end up covered up in paint?"

"I need to clean up before you dirty me up again." She wiggles her eyebrows. "You are going to dirty me up again?"

My cock hardens at her innuendo. He's all aboard the 'get Olivia dirty' train. He's not the only one.

I take her hand and lead her down the hallway. "You know water spillage is considered a crime in Winter Falls."

"It is?" She bats her lashes. "Whatever can we do to avoid committing this heinous crime?"

I pretend to consider the issue. "Well, if you cut the time you shower in half, it'd help."

She waves toward her body covered in paint. "I don't think I can shorten my shower time today."

"Hmm… maybe I can join you in the shower. If we both shower at the same time, we'll conserve water."

She sighs. All put out. "I guess if it's for the environment, I'm willing to sacrifice and share my shower with you."

I swallow my smile and feign being stern. "Are you sure? It is a big sacrifice."

She taps her chin. "I've considered it. I'm sure." She smirks before whipping her t-shirt off and racing away.

I catch her in the bathroom where she's managed to rid herself of her jeans in record time. I wrap my arms around her and pull her back to my front. "Do you think you can outrun me?"

She wiggles her ass and my cock jerks in anticipation. "Got ya in my bathroom, didn't I?"

I drag my teeth along her shoulder. She shivers in my arms, and I decide to push it. I sink my teeth into the juncture between her neck and shoulder and she practically melts in my arms. I soothe my tongue over the area and she moans.

I nibble on her earlobe. "Are you wet for me?"

"Of course, I'm wet. I'm covered in paint. Paint is a liquid."

I'm going to sex the sassy right out of her. I reach around to cup her over her underwear. She gasps and pushes into my hand.

I growl. "Don't move."

"What do I get if I stay still?"

Still sassy. Obviously, I need to work harder. I skim my finger over her panties to discover her soaking wet.

"I won't move," she breathes out.

I cup her again but leave my hand frozen there. I count to thirty before she starts to squirm.

"You said you wouldn't move."

"You said you would."

I thread my free hand through her hair before yanking her head back until she can meet my gaze. "Did I say I'd move?"

"No," she grumbles.

I tighten my hold on her hair and sparks ignite in her eyes. This woman is fucking perfect for me. I realize I didn't add the disclaimer 'in bed'. Is Olivia perfect for me full stop? Am I done falling? Have I fallen? Is she the woman I've been waiting for?

I study her face as she waits for me to proceed. She's gorgeous. Especially with my hand fisted in her hair. But it's not merely her looks or how she satisfies me in bed that has me contemplating if I love this woman.

She's also kind, a hard worker, loves her family, and is fun as hell. Fuck. It's true. I do love her. I file the information away for consideration later. For now, I've got a nearly naked woman in my arms who needs dirtying up.

"Good girl," I murmur before my hand delves inside her panties. "Spread your legs."

When she does, I reward her by sinking two fingers into her pussy. Her walls convulse around my fingers.

"You want to ride my hand?"

"Yes," she says and starts moving herself up and down on my fingers.

I pull her hair. "Stop. I didn't say you could ride my hand. I asked if you wanted to."

She grunts in frustration. "You're a tease."

"I'm a tease who's going to make you come so hard you see stars."

"Yes, please."

"Are you going to follow orders this time?"

Her walls flutter around my fingers. Someone enjoys being given orders.

She tries to nod but her head is immobilized. "Yes."

I grind the palm of my hand against her clit and she moans but remains still. She's earned a reward. "Ride my hand. Get yourself off."

Her hands grip my wrist as she follows my orders. I let go of her hair and trail my hand down her back to unclasp her bra. It falls down her shoulders to reveal her pretty pink nipples.

While she gets herself off using my fingers, I play with those nipples. I pinch and squeeze and twist them. Whenever I twist, her walls convulse around my fingers.

"Come for me now," I demand before pinching and twisting her nipple.

She clamps down on my fingers. "Yes. Yes. Yes."

I work my fingers in and out of her until her climax wanes. When she collapses, I free my hand and shove her panties down her legs.

"Now, it's my turn."

While I disrobe, Olivia switches on the water and hops in the shower. I'm happy to note she has a non-slip mat on the bottom of the shower as well as a bench seat across from the showerhead.

I join her and she immediately reaches for me. "You haven't kissed me yet."

I settle myself on the bench and she climbs on my lap. "You want my mouth?"

"It is a very nice mouth. I give it eight out of ten."

"How can I increase my score?"

She pretends to consider the question. "Maybe with a bit of practice. You know what they say. Practice, practice, practice will get you to—"

I bite her lip. "To come harder than you've ever come before."

Her eyes flare and her mouth opens to sass back at me, but I slam my mouth down on hers before she has the chance. She groans and palms my neck to pull me closer while I dig my fingers into the globes of her ass.

When I release her mouth, her lips are swollen, and her eyes are glazed over. She blinks and mischief appears in her gaze. "Guess what I can do?"

When I don't answer, she waggles her eyebrows. "I can do a handstand. It's very handy."

She stands and lifts her arms. I smack her ass. "Be careful. The floor is wet."

"I got this." She lunges forward and pushes off her back leg. I grab her leg as her hands hit the ground. She kicks the second leg off the ground and I grab it as well.

At the sight of her opened up for me, my cock twitches and I growl. "Wrap your legs around my waist," I order. "This is going to be hard and fast."

"Oh goodie." She winds her legs around me.

I don't waste any time thrusting into her. "Fuck. I'm deep."

She moans. "I noticed."

I freeze. "You okay?"

"Are we going to have the whole consent conversation again? After I did a handstand in the shower while naked?"

I slap her ass. "I meant did I hurt you."

"I'm going to hurt you if you don't start moving. How long do you think I can keep up this position?"

"Maybe we should—"

My words are cut off when she squeezes my cock with her inner muscles.

"Fuck. Fine."

I pull out before plunging into her again. We quickly find a rhythm with her pushing back on me while I thrust inside her. I get lost in the feel of her hot, wet walls surrounding me. My eyes shut and my head tilts back as I allow myself to just feel.

My world narrows to this shower with the woman I love and how unbelievable it feels to be inside her. The sound of skin slapping on skin echoes through the stall as water rains down on us.

"I'm coming," Olivia gasps before her walls clamp down on me with such force it throws me into my own climax.

"Livie!" I shout as I lose all pretense of rhythm.

Her arms wobble and I rush to lift her but my legs aren't steady yet and we collapse in a heap on the bottom of her shower.

She pushes her wet hair out of her face. "I don't think we saved any water."

I chuckle as I reach up to switch off the tap.

Chapter 27

Quiche – the breakfast of champions assuming you manage to actually finish baking it

✦

I GRUNT AS PEACE thrusts his hard length against my ass. I raech behind me to slap him.

"No. Go away. I'm sleeping."

He cuddles closer. "You didn't mind me waking you in the middle of the night."

It's true. I didn't. But I made him work for it. And I'm going to make him work for it this time, too. A man should have to work for his dessert.

"And now I'm sleep deprived."

"I bet I can get you to change your mind." His hand sneaks around our bodies until he can fondle my breasts.

I moan and thrust my chest into his hand. And – boom! – my mind is changed. I guess I didn't make him work for it after all.

Some time later I collapse against his chest. "I need a nap."

"It's ten o'clock in the morning. You can't take a nap now."

"Watch me," I grumble.

He shifts me off of his chest and rolls out of bed. I must fall asleep because the next thing I know he's strolling into the bedroom fully dressed with wet hair. He smacks me on the ass.

"Get up, sleepyhead."

"That's what she said."

He chuckles. "Get up or I won't make you breakfast."

I drag one eye open. "Breakfast?"

"Yep."

"What kind of breakfast?" If he says oatmeal or cereal, he can let himself out. I don't care if he's the man I love. Sunday breakfast does not consist of oatmeal or cereal.

"How about a quiche?"

Both of my eyes are open now. "With cheese?"

He chuckles. "Can you have a quiche without cheese?"

In my opinion, no, you cannot.

"You going to get your lazy out of bed?"

"Lazy?" I huff. "Riding you reverse cowboy is a freaking workout."

Every time I was about to come, he stopped. It was pure torture.

"If you wouldn't have played with those pretty titties of mine, I wouldn't have been forced to stop."

I glare at him. "These titties are mine. I remember when they arrived."

As you do when you're a late bloomer and your sister has you convinced you're going to be a negative A cup for the rest of your life.

"When we're in this bed, they're mine to play with, mine to torture, mine to fuck."

My breath hitches. "We haven't tried the last one yet."

His eyes flare. "You like the idea, don't you?"

Honestly, anything involving him and his naked body gets an automatic approval from me. But I'm not stupid enough to tell him anything of the sort.

I shrug. "I've never tried it before is all."

"Something to look forward to."

My nipples tingle in agreement. He smirks and steps toward me. My stomach chooses the moment to growl. Loudly.

"But first, breakfast."

"I don't have the ingredients to make a quiche," I shout after him. I wouldn't trust any eggs in my refrigerator.

"Don't worry. It's taken care of."

It is? How?

I scramble to my feet and throw on a t-shirt before rushing after him. Did he do groceries while I was sleeping? No, I wasn't asleep very long. He didn't have time.

When he opens the apartment door, I peek around him. There's a burlap bag in front of my door.

"Did you order groceries? I thought delivery services were banned in Winter Falls." I guess delivery services are bad for the environment. Don't ask me to explain. I don't understand most of the 'green' initiatives in this town.

He snatches the bag and shuts the door before walking to the kitchen to unpack the groceries.

"There isn't."

"Then, how did all of this end up on my doorstep?"

In response, he hands me a card. I rip it open and read aloud.

"Hope your night was as wild and crazy as your paint party. Enjoy your breakfast! Signed, The Gossip Gals. P.S. Please limit your use of water in the future."

I throw the card on the counter. "How the hell do they know about the shower?"

He chuckles as he searches the cabinets. "The same way they know everything happening in town," he says but doesn't elaborate.

"Which is?"

"Everyone in this town loves to gossip."

He finds a mixing bowl and a measuring cup and places the items on the counter before grabbing me around the waist and setting me on the counter.

"Keep me company."

I lift my arm and sniff my armpit. "I should probably shower."

He presses his nose against my throat and inhales. "I think you smell sexy."

"I think you mean I smell of sex."

"Sex. Sexy. Same thing."

He cracks an egg on the mixing bowl.

"Hold on." He halts with another egg in his hand to gaze up at me. "How did the gossip gals know you'd make me a quiche?"

I cross my arms over my chest and glare at him. "Is this what you make all your conquests?"

Crap. Here I am falling head over heels in love with the guy and I'm just another notch on his bedpost. My heart thumps in my chest and the only thing I can think of is to *flee.* I need to get the hell out of here. I push off of the counter, but Peace hems me in before I can jump.

"You are not some conquest," he growls.

I motion to the food laid out on the control. "But how?"

"This recipe is what I make every time I'm required to bring a dish somewhere."

My heart rate slows and hope builds. "It is?"

"Yeah, it is. I'm not in the habit of staying overnight at a woman's house."

"You aren't?"

He rubs his nose against mine. "No, Livie, I'm not."

"But you stayed here with me last night." He nods. "You didn't even ask if you could."

"Because I'm not stupid."

My brow wrinkles. "Why would asking be stupid?"

"I'm not an idiot. I'm not giving you a chance to retreat from me."

I don't know why he thinks I would retreat. I'm not a flighty girl. *Past Olivia* raises her hand and clears her throat. Oh. Right. I'm not a flighty girl anymore.

He rubs his hands up and down my thighs. "The quiche needs to bake for forty-five minutes. How about I get it prepped and in the oven and then we can fool around for forty-five minutes?"

I throw my arms around him. "You're obsessed with sex. Maybe you should see a counselor about your problem."

He growls. "My only problem is how irresistible you are."

I preen. "I am pretty irresistible, aren't I?"

"And humble. Don't forget humble."

"I'm not the one who claimed my cock is the king of the house."

He punches his hips until I feel his hard length against my belly. "Is this cock not the king of the house?"

He bunches up the material of my t-shirt until my nakedness is exposed.

"What is it with you and panties? Are you morally opposed to them?"

I wrap my legs around his waist. "They do tend to get in the way of what I want."

"I thought you wanted quiche."

"And I thought you were smarter."

He smirks before throwing me over his shoulder. He smacks my ass as he marches toward the bedroom. "I'm going to make you pay for your sass."

"Promise?"

"I've created a monster," he mumbles.

"Don't act like you don't love every second." I reach down to find his cock and squeeze it as hard as I can through his jeans and he moans.

"Your payment starts now," he declares as he throws me on the bed.

"I'll open up an account for you," I sass.

He barks out a laugh.

I have seriously never laughed and had this much fun in the bedroom before. Maybe it's because you love him, *New and Improved Olivia,* suggests. Nope, *Past Olivia* grunts. It's because he's a beast in the sack.

While the two voices in my head argue it out, I decide it's both. Peace is phenomenal in bed. He matches my sexual needs to a T. But he's also the man I love and I can't deny making love to the man you love is a whole different level of satisfaction.

Now I just need to figure out how I'm going to tell him I love him. I nearly blurted it out during sex several times last night, but I don't want him to think I'm moved by passion. I mean I am. But my love for him isn't the result of passionate sex.

Peace jumps on the bed and presses me into the mattress and I forget all about my fear of revealing my love to this man. I have better things to occupy my mind.

Chapter 28

Ambush – an unexpected surprise but not the good kind

❦

"WHAT IS ANCESTOR'S BLOB anyway?" I ask Peace as we walk into town from my apartment.

It's been a few weeks since the first time Peace stayed overnight in my apartment. Since then, he's spent more time in my apartment than in his. Although, with his twelve-hour shifts at the police station and my starting up a business, we're both busy people who aren't home much.

On another note, I haven't gathered the courage to tell him you know what. I've never confessed to loving a man before. I'm not clear on the rules.

Past Olivia snorts. And you're a big, fat chicken.

"It's Ancestors' Blot."

Peace's answer cleared things right up. Not.

"And? What is it?"

"Blot means celebration. Thus, today is a celebration of our ancestors."

"How do we celebrate our ancestors?"

"Mostly by stuffing our faces with food and drink."

"Sounds good to me."

We turn the corner toward Main Street and my mouth gapes open at the sheer amount of people milling about the town square.

"Is it always this crowded?" I don't remember Mabon being this crowded, although there was a ton of traffic when I drove into town for the Mabon festival.

"It's a bit more than usual," Peace begins and stops.

I motion for him to continue. "What?"

"I'm on call today."

I widen my eyes and slap my hands to my cheeks. "You don't say? You mean you're not wearing your uniform as a late Halloween costume?"

"Smart ass." He winds his arm around my neck and ruffles my hair.

I shove him away. "Don't ruin my hair."

"You're here," Ashlyn screams as she runs toward me. She grabs my hands and tries to pull me away.

"What's going on? Where are we going?"

Her best friend, Moon, appears behind her. "She wants to play whack-a-mole with you."

"You could have asked," I scold Ashlyn.

She juts out her bottom lip. "But no one wants to play with me."

Moon snorts. "Probably because you're a cheater."

Ashlyn widens her eyes. "I do not cheat."

I don't know her well but even I can tell she's lying.

"She totally cheats," Moon tells me. "She brings an extra hammer."

Ashlyn sniffs and lifts her chin. "It's not a hammer. It's a mallet."

"And it's cheating."

"Is not. Nowhere in the rules does it say you can't bring your own mallet."

Moon throws her arms in the air. "Because no one ever considered people might bring their own"

"It's not my fault I'm smarter than everyone else."

"Does this happen often?" I ask Peace as I motion toward the fighting friends.

"Ever since they became friends in kindergarten."

I step between them. "I'll play with you, Ashlyn." She beams in triumph. "If you promise to give your extra mallet to Peace while we play."

She juts her chin in the air. "Are you afraid I'll win?"

I roll my eyes. "It's not winning if you have two mallets and I have one."

"Are you going to be one of those people who say rules have to be followed?" I shrug. "And here I supported your acquisition of *Earth Bliss.*"

"Do you want to play or not?"

"Let's make this interesting," she says and Peace groans behind me.

"Interesting?"

"The loser has to take a turn in the dunk tank."

If she thinks she can scare me off, she's wrong. I may be the *New and Improved Olivia* but I still don't back down from, well, pretty much anything.

I hold out my hand. "You're on."

"I hope you brought dry clothes," she taunts before leading me toward the whack-a-mole game.

The participants notice her approach and lay down their mallets before leaving.

"Chickens," Ashlyn taunts after them.

She picks a spot and begins stretching her upper body.

"Ahem. Did you forget something?"

She bats her eyelashes. "I don't know what you mean."

"Surrender the mallet or our bet is null and void."

"Meanie," she mutters as she pulls the mallet out of the back pocket of her jeans and hands it to Peace.

Peace kisses my cheek. "Kick her ass."

"Yeah," Moon growls. "Kick her ass."

"Why is everyone against me?"

"Because you're a cheater!" Moon and I shout in unison.

And then the game begins to count down. I fist the mallet in my hand and concentrate on the holes where the moles pop out of. The first one pops out, but it's not a mole. I ignore my confusion and whack. I whack and whack and whack until the buzzer sounds.

My machine lights up and blares a siren. I won. I throw my hands in the air. "I won!" I point at Ashlyn. "You're a loser."

"Best two out of three."

High on my win, I don't hesitate to agree. "You're on."

The game begins counting down and I ready myself to whack the hell out of whatever these creatures are. They're certainly not moles.

When I win the second game, Ashlyn throws her mallet down. "This game is rigged."

"Someone's a sore loser," I tease.

"Best three out of five."

"Nope. You lost fair and square. It's time for the dunk tank."

"Ashlyn's going in the dunk tank," Moon yells before herding her friend away from the game and toward the town square.

I follow and Peace joins me. "Good job, Livie."

He kisses my hair and laces his fingers through mine as we walk down Main Street.

"What were those things anyway? They weren't moles."

"Oil rigs."

"Oil rigs?"

"Winter Falls," he says as if it's an answer. I guess when the town's claim to fame is being the first carbon neutral town in the world it is an answer.

"Whack-a-oil rig doesn't sound as good as whack-a-mole," I concede.

"Peace?" A woman calls.

"Fuck," he mutters under his breath.

"What's wrong? Do you need me to hide you? I've got a fast car. I don't have a plan to get us outta here, but I can make one up on the fly."

"Um," he hesitates.

A woman pushes her way through the crowd and stops in front of us.

"Too late now," I mutter.

"Peace," she says.

"Mom."

Mom? This is his mom? Crap on a cracker. I'm not ready to meet his mom. His hand tightens on mine as if he can sense I'm ready to flee. I wasn't going to run away. Pretending I need to use the bathroom and not returning is not running away FYI.

A man arrives and places his arm around Peace's mom. This must be his dad. Great. It's a two-for-one kind of day. I'm meeting his dad as well as his mom. What a bargain.

"Mom, Dad, this is Olivia. Oliva, these are my parents."

"Hi!" I wave with my left hand since someone is not letting my right hand go. "It's nice to meet you, Mr. and Mrs. Sky."

His dad grins. "It's Eagle and Clementine."

Clementine frowns at her husband. I guess she doesn't approve of me addressing her by her first name. Duly noted.

She crosses her arms over her chest and asks, "How long have you been dating?"

Oh boy. This isn't a friendly 'getting to know your son's girlfriend'-question. She's pissed at Peace. Damnit. I knew this was too good to be true. He's going to drop me faster than I can whack an oil rig because there's no way this woman is going to approve of me. The former troublemaker.

Let's burn her house down, Past Olivia suggests.

For the record, I have never actually burned someone's house down. I have no idea where she came up with the idea. Accidental fires do not count. Besides, who in their right mind leaves a can of gasoline lying around?

Peace clenches his jaw and a muscle ticks in his neck. Uh oh. Someone's pissed.

"I should…" I point vaguely to the other side of the street.

His hand clenches mine. "You're not going anywhere."

His mother scuffs. "Typical of an outsider. Ready to scamper away at the first sign of trouble."

Oh no, she didn't. My back straightens and my nose lifts. I open my mouth to blast her, but Peace gets there before I do.

"You will not speak to my girlfriend in this way."

Clementine rolls her eyes. "You know outsiders are not to be trusted."

Ding! Ding! Ding! The reason for Peace's distrust of outsiders is now clear. It was inherited. Good to know.

Peace leans forward to get in her face. "What I know is painting outsiders with the same brush is prejudiced."

I glance at Eagle. We need to do something. He shrugs as if he knows what I'm asking and has no ideas. A lot of good he is.

I decide to enter the arena. "I'm technically not an outsider."

Clementine's eyes narrow on me.

"I'm not. My brother's married to a local woman. One of my sisters manages the bar, *Electric Vibes.* Another of my sisters manages *Glitter N Bliss.*"

"How many sisters do you have?"

I know damn well she knows everything about me, but I pretend to take her question seriously.

"Three. The last sister is with Phoenix who owns a goat farm outside of town." I pause but she doesn't respond. "As you can see, I have numerous connections to Winter Falls."

"Plus, you're managing *Earth Bliss* now," Eagle adds.

I beam at him. "I am. Do you practice yoga?"

He opens his mouth to answer but his wife cuts him with a glare and he snaps his mouth shut.

"Mom," Peace says. "Olivia and I are together. Get used to it or don't expect me to come for Wednesday night dinner ever again."

New and Improved Olivia gets out the pompoms. *Yeah! He's sticking up for us. Past Olivia* sneers. *But for how long? He hasn't invited us to Wednesday dinner.*

"And I'll be bringing Olivia to dinner from now on."

New and Improved Olivia gloats at *Past Olivia. Told ya so.*

I don't share her enthusiasm. "Peace, I don't want to come in between you and your Mom."

I've caused enough trouble in my own family. I don't need to be causing it in other families, too.

He kisses my forehead. "You're not. Mom is getting in her own way."

Eagle clears his throat. "We'll see you next Wednesday." He shackles his wife's wrist and leads her away.

Peace runs a hand through his hair. "I'm sorry."

"Why are you apologizing?"

"My mom needs time. Once she warms up to you, she'll love you."

The way I love you? I manage to keep my mouth shut before the words slip out. Now is definitely not the time to declare my love to him.

"Okay. But now we need to go watch Ashlyn get dunked."

He chuckles as we make our way toward the town square.

Look at me negotiating my way out of a difficult situation. *New and Improved Olivia* nods in approval. *Past Olivia* rolls her eyes.

Chapter 29

Wishes – don't always turn out the way you want or expect

❧

PEACE

"Good morning," I greet Sage as I walk into the police station the next morning.

"Someone most definitely had a good morning." She smirks. "You're welcome."

I don't know why she's taking credit for my good mood. She had nothing to do with it. It was Olivia who woke me up with her hot mouth around my cock. She made it awful hard for me to leave her bed for my early morning shift.

"Aren't you going to thank me?"

"For what?" I ask, although I know exactly why she wants thanks.

"For matching you with Olivia."

"Nope. My relationship with Olivia has nothing to do with you and the gossip gals."

She gasps. "Peace Reed Sky! I changed your diapers."

This is her response whenever she's losing an argument and doesn't know how to dig herself out. I've long become immune to it.

I rap my knuckles on her desk. "Have a good morning, Sage," I say and walk off.

"Don't you dismiss me, Peace! I put you and Olivia together and you know it."

I pretend I don't hear her as I make my way down the hall to clock in for my shift and get my gear on.

"Peace," Sage calls over the radio and I nearly ignore her. But she usually doesn't mess around when it comes to the radio.

"Go ahead."

"There's a disturbance at *Naked Falls Brewing*."

"On my way."

I check my equipment before bounding out of the police station and down Main Street to the brewery. It's unusual for there to be trouble at the brewery at this time of the morning. Usually, Miller and Eden, the twin brothers who manage the brewery, aren't around until noon hits.

When I pass *Eden's Garden*, the flower shop owned by the current mayor, I hear shouting coming from behind the shop where Eden grows her plants. I debate continuing to the brewery but change direction when I hear Miller's voice.

I round the back of the flower shop to find Miller and Eden facing off with each other while Elder stands to the side.

"What's happening?" I ask Elder.

"The same thing that always happens whenever Eden and Miller are anywhere near each other."

Eden and Miller have never gotten along, but since the brothers applied to expand their brewery, their dislike for each other has turned into shouting matches in the street.

"Did you call in a disturbance?"

He frowns. "No. I can handle this."

Then, who did? I glance around the area. Clove, Feather, Cayenne, and Petal are standing on the other side of the garden. When they notice me, they wave. Dammit. They're up to their old tricks. They think they have me paired off now and it's time to move on to another victim.

I can't help but feel sorry for the two.

"I will never approve your plans," Eden shouts.

"You're supposed to be impartial," Miller yells back.

Maybe I don't feel sorry for them after all.

When I make my way to them, they don't even notice me. They're too busy trying to slay each other with the daggers shooting out of their eyes.

"I didn't ask to be mayor," Eden says.

"If you can't handle it, maybe you should resign."

Her nostrils flare and her hands fist at her hips. "Handle it? Do you think I can't handle it?"

He snorts. "Obviously."

Her teeth clench and I cringe at the grinding sound. She's going to need dentures if she keeps at it.

"Excuse me." Neither one of them bothers to glance in my direction.

"Leave them alone, Peace," Cayenne yells.

"They need to work this out on their own," Feather adds. "Preferably between the sheets."

"I need to make a new batch of candles," Petal says.

Clove giggles. "Those two do not need candles."

Feather nods in agreement. "The looks they're giving each other could light a forest fire without a match."

I step to the side to block their view of Eden and Miller and they boo. The booing attracts Eden's attention. She notices the gossip gals and rolls her eyes.

"You are not matching me with Miller the plant killer," she snarls.

"Enemies to lovers is my favorite," Feather shouts back.

Miller scoffs. "As if Eden could handle me."

"What is it with you thinking I can't handle things? Think again. I would wipe the floor with you."

He gets in her face. "Bring it on, plant lady. Bring it on."

"All right. All right." I step between them. "Enough."

"Come on, Peace. You know as well as I do these outsiders do not belong in Winter Falls."

I cringe. What kind of asshole have I been in the past to make Eden think I'll automatically take her side just because Miller and Elder didn't grow up in Winter Falls?

"Eden," I warn. "Elder and Miller have been in Winter Falls for years. They've built up a nice business, which brings visitors to town. They're not some tourists gawking at our beliefs for entertainment."

Her eyes narrow at me. "When did you change your tune?" She sighs. "Oh right. Olivia."

I'm not defending Elder and Miller because of Olivia, but I can't deny the woman confronted my views on out-of-towners and proved I was being a bit of a dick, although she'd use a much stronger word starting with ass and ending with hole.

Miller crosses his arms over his chest. "Poor Eden. Even the local cops won't come to her rescue."

I point at him. "Watch what you say to her while I'm around."

"Oh no, the local fuzz is terrifying me."

Does he think he'll get a rise out of me? Ha! I've heard much worse in my years of being a police officer. Working in a small town doesn't necessarily mean I've been saved from poor treatment by the locals.

"Don't give Peace a hard time," Elder orders as he approaches.

"There you go again. Always coming to his defense. I'm the brother you grew up with. You should be on my side."

Brother he grew up with? What an odd turn of phrase.

"Yeah, well, he's the brother we moved here to get to know and yet you haven't made any effort to get to know him in the past five years."

"Hold up. What are you talking about?"

Elder jerks backwards. "Shit. I forgot you were standing there."

"Explain yourself because it sounded an awful lot like you think I'm your brother."

"Not think. Know," Miller says.

What the hell? I don't have any siblings. My parents didn't have any children after me. Am I adopted? Have my parents lied to me for my entire life?

"What's going on?" Petal shouts and I jolt. Shit. We're standing out in the open where anyone can eavesdrop.

"We can't hear you," Feather adds.

Fuck. I need to get a handle on this situation before the gossip gals start spreading rumors about my family. Nasty rumors since they can't possibly be true.

I point to Eden. "You. You will review the plans for the expansion of the brewery with an open mind."

She raises her hands in the air and backs away. "Okay."

"And you two are going to explain yourselves." I motion to the brewery. "In private."

"Where are you going?" Clove yells after us but I ignore her. This has nothing to do with the gossip gals. Not everything that happens in Winter Falls is their business, no matter what they think.

Miller opens the door to the brewery and I follow him and Elder inside. I scan the area to check if anyone else is around before I lock the door behind me.

"What the hell are you saying?" I ask. "I'm not your brother."

"Half-brother," Elder clarifies.

"Are you certain you want to do this?" Miller asks Elder. "He's obviously not ready."

I don't wait for Elder to respond. "Too late now. We're doing this."

"Your father is our father," Elder says.

"Eagle is your father?"

Miller shakes his head. "No, and he isn't your father either."

I growl. "Eagle sure as hell is my father."

"Not your biological father," he clarifies.

"Are you saying my mother cheated on my father? No way," I scoff.

Mom is as devoted to Dad as he is to her. I've always envied their close relationship. Can my mom be a little quick to judge? Yeah, she can. But once she's on your side, she's devoted for life.

"We don't know the whole story," Elder claims, but his eyes darting to the side make him a liar.

"How did you find me if you don't know the story?"

"We did one of those genealogical kits."

"No one was more surprised than us when we got a possible match for a sibling," Miller adds.

I latch onto his words. "Possible sibling? This could be some mistake. We could be cousins or a distant relative."

"Actually, we're certain."

How can they be certain if they don't know the whole story? They're withholding information from me.

My radio squawks. "Peace, we need you back at the station."

I sincerely doubt it. What Sage *wants* is all the gossip. She's not getting it, but her call is as good an excuse as any to leave since I'm not ready to process the possibility of having a family I knew nothing about.

No, it's not a possibility. They can't be my brothers. Mom would never cheat on Dad. I know she wouldn't.

"We'll discuss this later," I tell Miller and Elder and march away without waiting for a response.

Chapter 30

Mistake – an excuse to avoid the truth

🦋

"WHAT CRAWLED UP YOUR ASS?"

Peace shrugs. "I don't know what you're talking about."

I snort. "Liar. You're upset about something."

I'd be stupid not to notice. He's sitting on my couch, but he hasn't paid a bit of attention to the movie on the television. His eyes are too busy darting around the room while he drums his fingers on his thigh.

"It's complicated."

Which is code for 'I don't trust you enough to tell you'. The man I love doesn't trust me. Ouch! *You obviously don't trust him either. Why else haven't you admitted you love him? New and Improved Olivia* is a pain in my ass.

I rein in *Past Olivia* who wants to kick his balls up his scrotum if he won't tell us what's going on. She's feisty and mean. Mostly mean.

I stand. "Scooch forward."

He frowns at me but slowly moves forward until he's sitting on the edge of the couch, and I climb in behind him. I dig my fingers into his shoulders and begin to massage his muscles.

"Wow. You are major tense. I guess early morning blow jobs don't have any lasting effect."

He chuckles. "Sorry. Work was a bitch."

"I hear you. During today's Hatha yoga class, Clove announced she can do the splits. I don't know why. We don't do the splits in Hatha yoga. But she was determined to show everyone. Spoiler alert. She can't do the splits. She got stuck midway and we had to help her up."

"She used to be able to do the splits."

"And how do you know this tidbit of information?"

"Clove used to coach the cheerleading squad. Actually," he pauses, "she wasn't the appointed coach. She would just show up and start coaching."

I giggle. "Why am I not surprised?"

I knead his shoulders and his head falls back on a moan. "This feels fabulous."

"As good as your 'welcome to the work week' blow job?"

His eyes fly open and his gaze meets mine. "I think you know the answer to that question," he growls.

"It doesn't hurt to check."

"I'm not ready to talk about it."

"But you admit something's bothering you. I was right. I win."

"You're a fruitcake."

"We've discussed this. I can't be a fruitcake when I'm not soaked in alcohol." He smiles and I continue to work his shoulders. "You're very tense."

Hint. Hint. Tell me what's going on.

His eyes fall closed again and he leans back against me. "If only there was a way to relieve my stress."

"If you're hinting for an after work blowjob, you're out of luck. The casserole will be finished soon and I'm hungry."

"What if I'm hungry for a non-food item?"

I slap his shoulder before returning to his massage. "You'll have to wait like a good little boy."

His voice lowers. "But you enjoy it when I'm bad."

Hell yeah, I do. I more than enjoy it. I freaking love it. The way I love him.

Tell him! Tell him! Crap on a cracker. *Past Olivia* and *New and Improved Olivia* have teamed up. This will not end well for me.

"Did you have to arrest a lot of people today?" I ask and both Olivias boo me and call me a coward.

"In Winter Falls? Nah. But Eden and Miller had a huge fight I had to break up."

"Eden the mayor?"

"The one and only."

"This town is awesome," I declare. "Where else does a cop have to break up a fight the mayor's involved in?"

"You're trouble."

"Nope. I'm fun." I kiss his forehead. "What were they fighting about anyway?"

"Eden doesn't want the brewery expansion to go through. She was screaming at Miller about it. Elder was there, too."

He frowns. I draw a finger down his forehead where a deep wrinkle forms.

"There's more to it than you're telling me."

He nods. "There is," he confirms, although he didn't need to.

I've known something was up with him the minute he charged into my apartment with his nostrils flaring and raring for a fight. A fight I refused to give him despite *Past Olivia* egging me on. I handed him a beer, chose a movie, and shoved him onto the couch.

"You don't have to tell me but promise me something."

"What?" he asks, his voice full of suspicion.

I ignore the pain his obvious distrust of me causes. This moment is not about me. *Past Olivia* pouts. *It's always about me.*

"Promise me you'll find someone to talk to."

He scowls.

"I don't mean a therapist. I mean a friend. You have a lot of anger bottled up inside of you. It's not good for your blood pressure."

He waggles his eyebrows. "I know what will help lower my blood pressure."

I smack his shoulder. "I'm serious."

He sighs and returns his gaze to the television. "Who am I going to talk to?"

I give up on the massage and return to my spot in the corner of the couch. "A friend? A colleague? A mentor?"

Yeah, yeah, I realize how much of a hypocrite I am. I can't count the number of times someone – usually of the sister variety – pressed me to find a person to confide in and I ignored them. I was wrong. Peace can learn from my mistakes. I sure didn't.

"Anyone I talk to will run their mouth and the news will be all over town in a matter of minutes."

"Come on. There has to be someone in town who isn't a gossip. What about your boss, Lyric?"

"He'll tattle to his wife, Aspen, who will gossip to her sisters and before you know it – boom! The whole town thinks my mom's a cheater."

I debate asking him what he means. He didn't intend to spill his secrets to me after all. On the other hand, spilled milk can't be saved.

"Cheater?"

"Fuck!" he shouts and jumps to his feet. He paces around the living room while running his hands through his hair.

I hold my hands up in surrender. "It's okay. I don't need to know." I clear my throat. "I'm here, though, if you want to talk." The 'if you trust me' is left unspoken.

He stares at the floor for several minutes. Until I'm convinced the conversation is over. I ignore how his lack of trust causes my chest to tighten to the point of pain. Not about me, I remind myself.

I've given up on him speaking when his eyes meet mine and he confesses, "Elder and Miller claim I'm their half-brother."

Whoa! Those are not the words I expected him to speak. "Your dad had other children?"

"No. They claim the man who raised me is not my father."

Whether Eagle donated his sperm to Peace or not, he is Peace's father. He raised him and he obviously loves him. But now isn't the moment to discuss biological versus adoptive parents.

"How could they possibly know this?"

"They did one of those genealogical home tests and my name came up as a possible sibling."

"And they're just telling you now? How long have they lived in Winter Falls?"

"A few years. I get the feeling Elder wanted to tell me, but Miller didn't."

"But they told you today?"

"Elder accidentally let it slip. When I questioned him, the story came out."

"How certain are they?"

"They're certain."

"They could have made a mistake," I suggest. I have no idea how accurate those home genealogical tests are.

"Exactly!"

"Or it could be right."

He huffs. "My mom would never have an affair. I know she wasn't exactly warm and friendly to you." Gross understatement. "But once she accepts you, she'll defend you until her dying breath."

We're not discussing my relationship with his mother now. I'll be avoiding *that* topic until the goats come home.

"You need to talk to her. Ask her why Miller and Elder would claim to be your step-brothers."

"It's a waste of time. It's all bullshit."

"What if it's not? What if you have another family out there?"

"I told you it's bullshit."

I flinch at the anger in his voice but I am not giving up on this. "I would do anything – anything – to get the past two years without my family in my life back. And my parents." My voice wobbles and I clear my throat before powering on. "I would give up my life to see them one more time. One more kiss on my cheek from Mom. One more ruffle of my hair from Dad."

My eyes itch and I blink fast to stop the tears from rolling down my face but it's no use. The dam breaks.

"Fuck, Livie."

Peace draws me into his arms and sways me from side to side. "I'm sorry. I didn't think how discussing family would affect you."

"You want to apologize properly? Confront your mom and find out the truth."

"I hate when you're right."

"You better get used to it because I'm not going anywhere."

"Thank fuck," he mutters before his lips crash down on mine and there's no more discussion of families and possible betrayals.

There's only me and Peace and the feeling of his hands on me, his mouth devouring mine, the anticipation of what's to come. The casserole is completely forgotten.

Chapter 31

Blame – when you're too chickenshit to take responsibility for your actions

+

"Hello, my dear boy. I didn't know you were stopping by today."

Yeah, well, neither did I. But Olivia's tears as she wished for more time with her deceased parents keep playing on my mind. On top of which, she hasn't stopped asking me when I'm going to talk to my mom. She's relentless.

This does not bode well for my future. I shove those thoughts out of my mind. Today isn't about the future. It's about the past.

I kiss my mom's cheek and she ushers me inside.

"Is Dad around?"

"Am I not enough for you?" she teases.

"I guess. If you have coffee."

"I have coffee and I made a coffee cake this morning."

"You know the way to a man's heart."

I frown. Is Dad's heart the only one she's known?

"Uh oh. What's wrong?"

I wipe the frown from my face. "What do you mean? What could be wrong?" Besides everything.

"You have that wrinkle you get on your forehead when you're upset."

I slap a hand over my forehead as if I can hide the evidence of how upset I am after she's already seen it.

"Sit down. I'll get you a coffee and a big slice of coffee cake."

I won't say no to either one of those. Even if my stomach feels as if I went on a tequila bender last night.

I sit at the kitchen table while Mom prepares my coffee and cake. I fist my hands to stop myself from burying my face in them. I want to hide from this conversation. I want to run away and pretend Miller and Elder never claimed to be my brothers.

"Is it Olivia?" Mom asks as she sits across from me.

"Is what Olivia?"

"Is Olivia the reason you appear ready to throw your coffee in my face?"

I latch onto the excuse to delay discussing Mom's alleged fidelity issues.

"She's not, but as long as you brought up the subject…" I let my words hang; hoping she'll charge in and apologize.

"You caught me by surprise." This isn't sounding much like an apology. "I didn't expect you to date an outsider."

"First of all, Olivia isn't an outsider. Second, who cares if she is? She makes me happy." And I love her. I keep the confession to myself. I haven't told Olivia I love her yet and she deserves to be the first person I say those words to.

"But you don't like outsiders."

I growl at the reminder of what an asshole I was to Olivia when she first came to town.

"You've never liked them." She crosses her arms over her chest. "Don't you remember how you fought the establishment of the brewery because it would be operated by two outsiders?"

Thanks for the opening, Mom.

"Two outsiders such as Miller and Elder?"

"Exactly."

"What if they aren't outsiders?"

Her nose wrinkles. "What do you mean? Naturally, they're outsiders. They weren't born and raised in Winter Falls."

"What if they're related to someone in town? Would they be outsiders then?"

"If they were related to someone in town, we would have known them before they showed up here all of sudden demanding to start a business."

I sip on my coffee as I gather the courage to say the next bit.

"Miller and Elder claim to be related to someone in town," I say with my gaze focused on my coffee cup.

"Ha! Who?"

I lift my head until my eyes meet hers. "Me."

Her eyes widen and her hand flies to her chest. "You?" The word comes out strangled.

"Yes, me. They claim to be my half-brothers."

She sways in her chair before clutching the table to steady herself. "Your half-brothers?"

I nod.

"Your half-brothers?" she repeats.

"What the hell is going on here?" Dad shouts as he rushes to Mom and gathers her in his arms. "What did you do to your mother?"

No way. He's not blaming me for this shit show. This is all on her cheating ass.

"He found out." At Mom's soft whisper, Dad's eyes close as his chin falls to his chest.

A heavy feeling settles in my stomach as I realize it's true. Mom's a cheater and Dad's not my dad and Miller and Elder are my brothers. Son of a bitch. My entire life is a lie.

Dad's the first to recover. He clears his throat. "Let's discuss this in the living room."

He carries Mom to the sofa and sets her down before kissing her forehead. "Everything will be all right. I promise you."

I follow and collapse in the armchair. Dad presses a cold beer into my hand. "Too early for whisky."

I have a feeling it's never too early for whisky when you learn you have a family you know nothing about. Speaking of which.

"How could you keep this from me? You know I've always wanted siblings, but you refused to consider giving me a brother or sister."

"Son," Dad's voice rumbles in warning.

"Son? I'm not your son, though, am I?" I lash out.

"You are my son," he insists. "I was there when you were born and have loved and cared for you from that moment on. I know you're shocked, and your world has been tipped upside down. You can go ahead and scream, shout, and yell. Hell, break shit if you need to. But don't you dare say I'm not your dad."

I thread my hands through my hair and pull.

"But how? How are you not my dad?" He growls. "My biological dad?"

"Clementine? This is your story to tell. If you want to."

If she wants to? I don't give a flying crap what she wants. I'm thirty-five years old and my entire life has been a lie. I want the truth.

Mom wrings her hands as she stares at the ground with her mouth firmly shut. I stand. If she won't tell me what happened, I'll find someone who will. I deserve the truth.

"Sit down," Dad orders. "She needs a damn minute."

I concentrate on the *tick tock* of the kitchen clock as I wait for Mom to gather her nerves. Five minutes pass before she finally speaks.

"When your father and I were dating before you were born, he said he needed a break."

"Because I'm an idiot," Dad butts in to say.

Mom ignores his interruption. "I thought break meant the end. I loved him with all my heart and he didn't feel the same." She sniffs and Dad wraps her in his arms.

"She left. She went on a vacation in California," Dad takes over the narrative.

"And I got drunk and slept with a guy I barely knew." She blushes but manages to carry on telling her tale. "When I woke up in a place I didn't recognize, I realized I was out of control and returned home."

"Where I was waiting to apologize." Dad smiles down at her.

"We made up and everything was perfect." She pauses. "Except for two months later when I realized I was pregnant."

"Which was the moment I had to admit to her the reason I wanted a break."

"Which was?" I ask when Dad doesn't continue.

"I can't have children. When I found out, I pushed Clementine away. I wanted her to have everything she's ever wanted, and she's always wanted a big family."

"So when she wound up pregnant, you stayed with her?"

He smiles down at Mom. "Of course. I love her. She didn't cheat on me. She made a drunken mistake when she was heart-broken."

"But what about my dad?"

"He's sitting right here."

I wave away his protest. "I mean my biological dad. Who is he? Where is he? Why didn't you ever tell me about him?"

"I searched for him. I promise you I did. But I couldn't find him. This was in a time before the internet and Google. The only thing I knew about him was his first name. I didn't know where he lived. Where his family was from. What he did for a job. Nothing."

I guess they skipped the getting to know you portion of the evening and went straight to— Ew. I squash those thoughts. I don't need to have pictures of my mom having an affair with some boy in my mind. Yuck.

Mom clears her throat and sits up straight. "Can you forgive me? I know it was wrong to keep this from you, but I didn't think telling you would help since I didn't know who your father was anyway."

I rub a hand over my face. "I don't know, Mom. Things have changed. I understand you couldn't find my biological dad back in the day, but now? I could probably figure out who he is easily enough."

"But you don't need to," Dad says.

"What do you mean?"

"You can ask Miller and Elder who he is. Find out everything you want to know about him. Maybe even meet him."

Mom gasps. "You want to meet him?"

I shrug. I don't know. I don't know anything at the moment. The only thing I know is that my parents have lied to me since the moment I was born.

I stand. "I need time to think." I make my way toward the door.

My parents follow me. "Please don't hate me," Mom begs.

"I don't hate you." But I am really, really pissed at her at the moment. I keep those feelings to myself, though, since Dad's standing there ready to slay me for the first wrong thing to come out of my mouth.

If he loves her and forgives her, maybe I can, too. In time. I need time.

Chapter 32

Excuse – there isn't always one. End of discussion.

I MARCH UP THE stairs toward the courthouse and the police station within. I am a woman on a mission. Peace has been ignoring me for a week now. And I am over it.

And by ignore, I mean I haven't seen him since the morning he left my apartment the day after he learned he has a family he had no idea existed. Not okay. We're in a relationship. It may be one of my first serious relationships – which is totally embarrassing to admit at the age of thirty-five – but I will not fail. Not when I love the man.

I pause with my hand on the doorknob. Maybe not seeing each other for a week is normal for relationships? Maybe I'm exaggerating the situation? Maybe he's just busy the way he claims?

Nope. I will not doubt myself. He doesn't work seven days a week. And this is a small town. It's not as if he's investigating murders or egregious crimes. He can spare fifteen damn minutes to have a coffee with me.

The second I open the door I hear fighting. Huh. Maybe he is busy and isn't avoiding me.

Sage tuts. "I thought he found out long ago."

Hold on. What is she saying? "Knew what?"

"Don't play innocent with me. I know you know."

I'm not playing. I'm ascertaining how much she knows before I spill the beans. I promised Peace I can keep a secret. And I darn well will.

"Know what?"

"About his family."

I glare at her. "You knew about Miller and Elder?"

She shrugs. "I suspected."

"And you didn't think to say anything? You sat there on your throne and waited for Peace to be devastated?"

She smiles. "I knew we were right about you."

I growl. "Don't you dare give me any of your matchmaking bullshit right now. I want answers. You knew the brewery twins were his brothers?"

"No. But I did know Eagle isn't his biological father. Everyone knows."

Hold up. "Everyone knows?" Peace sure as hell didn't know.

"Yep."

"Everyone knows and no one ever said a thing to him?"

I find this hard to believe. This is Winter Falls where it's impossible to keep a secret. A secret this juicy would have leaked ages ago.

"We were waiting for Clementine to tell him."

But Clementine didn't tell him. Instead, he was blindsided by Miller and Elder.

"You're unbelievable."

She preens. "Thank you."

"It wasn't a compliment."

She winks. "I disagree."

"If you steal my energy drink one more time, I'm going to cut you," Peace shouts.

Sage motions toward the shouting. "You better get in there and save the day."

I'm not saving the day, but I will save Peace from himself. I march into the main area of the police station to find Peace and Freedom facing off. Peace's nostrils flare while he fists his hands at his sides.

"What's going on here?"

Freedom glances over his shoulder at me and the tension leaves his body. "Someone's throwing a temper tantrum."

"I'm not throwing a temper tantrum," Peace denies. "I'm calling you out for stealing my stuff."

"Dude, I always borrow your energy drinks. And, afterwards, I refill the stock."

Are they serious? "You're fighting over Red Bull?"

Freedom rears back. "Red Bull? In Winter Falls? No way. Gracious, over at the diner makes these energy drinks. They taste like fruit juice but will keep you awake during a midnight shift without making you jittery. They're the bomb."

"You can buy your own damn drinks from Gracious and stop stealing mine," Peace grumbles.

"Dude, what crawled up your ass and died? You've been a bear for a week." Freedom nods to me. "Sort him out. I'm out of here."

I wait until Freedom's gone before addressing Peace, "Are you okay?"

"Fine," he says but looks everywhere but at me.

If this is fine, I don't want to see how bad looks.

"How have you been? I haven't seen you in a week."

"Is this when you become the clingy girlfriend?" he snarls. "Because I won't tolerate it."

Kick him in the gonads, Past Olivia shouts. Meanwhile, *New and Improved Olivia* balls herself up in the corner and starts crying. Some help she is.

I raise my hands in surrender. "Even without Lilac, I know the definition of clingy and I am not it."

He runs a hand through his hair and grunts. I hope a grunt isn't his idea of an apology because it doesn't fly with me.

"I was worried about you."

"Me too!" Sage shouts from where she's now standing at the end of the hallway.

"You told her? What the hell, Olivia? You promised you'd keep your big mouth shut."

Big mouth? So much for him trusting me. I shackle his wrist and drag him to the interrogation room.

Once we're behind a shut door, I turn on him. "I haven't told anyone anything."

He narrows his eyes and studies me as if he doesn't believe me. No need to wonder whether he trusts me any longer. The answer is no. Effing ouch.

"It certainly sounds as if Sage knows what's happening."

Shit. Damn. Fuck. Crap. He's going to be pissed when he hears what she knows. Considering he's already pretty pissed, he may in fact explode. Great.

Tell him, Past Olivia pushes. *Tell him and make him explode. This is what he gets for not trusting us.*

I hate to listen to *Past Olivia*. Talk about a bad influence. But he needs to know.

"The older generation in Winter Falls know Eagle isn't your father."

"This is what I get for falling for an outsider. The second you had a chance to run your mouth off you went."

I fist my hands on my hips before I deck him. Something both Olivias are in favor of at the moment.

"They all knew!" I shout.

He freezes. "What?"

"According to Sage, the older generation all know about Eagle not being your biological dad. They kept their mouths shut because they were giving Clementine the opportunity to confess to you herself."

He rubs his hand over his jaw where a few days of beard growth is visible. Shit. If he's not shaving, he's really hurting.

I reach for him. "They're not trying to hurt you, Peace."

He yanks his hands free from mine. "They may not be trying, but they sure as hell are."

I lift my hands and retreat a few steps. Obviously, he doesn't want comfort from me. A dagger pierces my heart at the thought of the man I love hurting and not wanting me to be there for him, but I ignore it. This moment is about him. Not me.

Screw him, Past Olivia shouts. *Teach him a lesson!*

I'm tempted to follow her advice. Not a good sign. I inhale a cleansing breath before I lash out at Peace. Lashing out will help no one in this situation.

"They care about you."

"How would you know?" he snarls. "What do you know about people caring for each other? You abandoned your family for two years."

This time when *Past Olivia* rears her head, I let her take the reins. Fuck Peace. I will not have my past thrown at me because he's hurting.

"Screw you. You need to grow the eff up. This entire town is waiting to catch you as you fall and you snarl and shout at them. You're an idiot."

I march to the door and yank it open.

"There you go, little girl. Run away when the going gets tough."

I pause with my hand on the door handle. Is he right? Am I running away?

"You have no staying power anyway. You'll never make a go of the yoga studio. At the first sign of trouble, off you'll go. It must be nice having mommy and daddy's money to fall back upon."

Wow. I can't believe I fell in love with this asshole. Yeah, he's hurting but there are some lines you don't cross. Ever. And bringing up my dead parents and their money didn't merely cross the line, it jumped over to the next stratosphere.

"We're done," I tell the door.

"Of course, we are," Peace says and any hope I was holding onto of him fighting for us up and disappears. He is not the man I thought he was.

Stupid, stupid, Olivia. Falling for the first man to show her a bit of kindness.

I charge out of the room and smack dab into Lyric's arms. "Olivia, what's wrong?"

"Why would anything be wrong?"

"You're crying and choking for breath."

I swipe at the tears I hadn't noticed flowing down my face.

"I'm fine," I claim and sprint away from him. I push past Sage and race out of the police department. I don't stop until I reach my apartment where I collapse.

Let's get drunk and slash his tires, Past Olivia suggests. I'm tempted. Seriously tempted. Peace is lucky he doesn't own a car.

Chapter 33

❧

"Huh. Do you think she cried herself to sleep?"

Cassandra's question wakes me – crap, I did cry myself to sleep – and I open my eyes to discover all three of my sisters standing over me.

"This is the creepiest way I've ever been woken up," I mutter as I rub my eyes.

Cassie beams down at me. "You're welcome."

Welcome? Is she crazy? I should be thanking her for creeping me out? I think not. But there are more important things to discuss, such as, "How did you get inside my apartment?"

Elizabeth rolls her eyes. "Each of us has a key."

Cassandra elbows her. "You promised me you didn't keep a key when I moved in."

Remind me never to move into an apartment my sisters have lived in before me again. "Let me guess. There's not a locksmith in town."

"Phoenix can change the lock for you," Gabrielle offers.

I raise my eyebrows. "And you won't keep a spare key?"

She shrugs. "You have to admit it's necessary for situations such as this one."

My brow wrinkles. "Situations such as this one? You mean the three of you invading my space?"

Elizabeth rolls her eyes. "No. The three of us coming to comfort you when your heart is broken."

At the reminder of why I cried myself to sleep, my heart squeezes and I rub my chest to alleviate the pain. Damn it. News travels fast in this town.

Cassie pushes my legs off of the sofa before sitting down. Yes, I fell asleep on the sofa. In my defense, the bedroom smells of Peace. And, no, I didn't sniff the sheets like some whiney heartbroken teenager. For long.

Cassie pats my leg. "I brought ingredients to make cocktails."

A cocktail would hit the spot, but I'm not giving in this easily. "I don't need you to comfort me."

"Too bad. We're here," she says and Gabrielle and Elizabeth nod in agreement.

"You should be happy we—"

I cut Elizabeth off before she can continue. "Happy?" I sneer. "I should be happy the man I love kicked me to the curb without a second thought? Your definition of happy is completely whacked."

"You love Peace?" Cassie asks.

I roll my eyes. "Of course, I do. He's perfect."

"And a cop."

"I know, but I've decided to forgive him for his bad taste in career choice."

But the forgiveness stops there. I won't be forgiving him soon for the things he said today. No way. I deserve to be treated better.

Beckett drummed it into us as teenagers. You have to demand respect from a man. And you never allow a man to treat you like shit. It might have taken me a minute for me to get with the program, but I'm there now.

Speaking of big brother. "Beckett isn't off beating Peace up now, is he?"

I may think the guy is a rat sewer, but I still love him and don't want him hurt. I guess Cassie hasn't cornered the market on crazy.

"Beckett and Lilac are at a convention in Seattle," Gabrielle says.

Phew. The last thing I need is to bail big brother out of jail for beating up a cop. Although, the irony of it would be hilarious. The gag gifts at Christmas would be never ending. Huh. Maybe Beckett should beat up Peace after all. Peace would recover.

"They have lots of business to attend to," Elizabeth adds.

"I think she means they need to do the business." Cassie wiggles her eyebrows.

I groan and cover my head with the blanket. "I'm never going to have sex again," I wail.

Cassie pulls the blanket away. "Why? Are your parts broken?"

"No. Can your parts down there break?"

"Sometimes it feels as if they do," Elizabeth mutters.

"Seriously?" I snap at her. "You're bragging about how awesome River is in bed when I'll probably end up celibate for the rest of my life? Maybe I should join a convent."

"You could become a priest in India. Don't they enjoy yoga?"

I throw my pillow at her. "I'm not living in India. I thought you wanted me to live near you."

I may sound the teeniest tiniest bit uncertain.

"I want you here." She launches herself at me but hits her knee on the coffee table and ends up in a heap on the floor at my feet.

"There's no need to worship me," I tell her. "I'm not a priest."

"I can't believe I canceled movie night with River for this," she mutters.

"What is this anyway?" I ask. "Why are you here?"

My sisters have never shown up at my apartment as a group before. *Probably because you avoided them in Saint Louis, New and Improved Olivia* reminds me.

"I told you. To comfort you," Cassie says.

"And reminding me I'm never going to have sex again is comfort how?"

Gabrielle's face flames and she tucks her chin into her chest. "I brought food."

I point to the bag I didn't notice her carrying. "If there's chocolate in there, you're forgiven."

She snorts. "Duh."

"You're forgiven." I can be magnanimous. I point to Elizabeth. "Whatcha got? Besides a bad case of the klutz."

She crosses her arms over her chest and huffs. "I am not a klutz."

"Did you forget how you tripped at Lilac's wedding and took down three people with you like they were human bowling pins?"

Cassie raises her hand. "I didn't forget."

"It's hard to forget when there's photographic evidence," Gabrielle adds.

"Fine. Say I'm a klutz. See if I let you watch any of the movies I brought."

I slap my palms against my cheeks. "Oh no. Whatever will I do? How will I survive with a mere five streaming services to provide me with entertainment?"

"Joke's on you. I got the movies from Juniper."

"Juniper as in Maverick Langston's fiancée?" I cross my fingers. "New romantic comedy with Maverick. New romantic comedy with Maverick."

"Say I'm not a klutz and we'll watch it."

I'm not saying shit. I snatch her bag from the floor where it landed when she fell. "Victory is mine!" I raise my hands in the air.

Elizabeth lunges at me and I spring to my feet before jumping over the back of the sofa and running toward the kitchen.

"Don't make me chase you. I still owe you for the paint incident."

I whirl around on her. "Owe me? It's my fault you tripped on a can of paint?"

"You deliberately put the can where I would trip over it."

"Because I'm psychic and know everywhere you're planning to walk? This is a sucky psychic power. If I'm psychic, I want to know lottery numbers. Screw messing with my sister."

"Fine." She slumps into an armchair. "You can watch the movie."

"How magnanimous of you to allow me to watch the movie you brought into my home for me to watch."

Cassie stands from the sofa. "I better start mixing the cocktails."

"What time is it anyway?"

"Not yet eight."

Not yet eight? I thought I'd been asleep for hours. Note to self: crying your eyes out is exhausting and messes with your sense of time.

"What are you making?"

"Jalapeno margaritas."

"Tequila. Good choice."

"Speaking of which." She motions for Gabrielle and Elizabeth to join us before she pours four shots of tequila and hands them out.

"Are you sure tequila shots are a good idea?" Elizabeth asks.

"Tequila shots are always a good idea when you're heartbroken," Cassie says.

"I guess you don't remember the time Olivia got drunk on tequila shots and decided to confront the neighbor."

"Hey!" I shout. "I caught him peeping in our bedroom window. Not okay."

"Agreed, but you probably should have confronted him when you were sober because drunk Olivia knocked him out."

I dip my chin so she can't see the smug expression on my face. Our neighbor in Saint Louis was over six-foot tall and about as wide. I still can't believe I knocked him on his ass with one punch.

"He deserved it."

"You broke his nose."

I know. Blood spurted everywhere when I hit him. It was magnificent. Too bad I didn't film it.

"Blame Beckett. He's the one who insisted we attend those self-defense classes."

Gabrielle's nose wrinkles. "I don't remember learning how to punch in those classes."

"It was the advanced class," I lie.

"Liar!" Cassie points at my neck, which I happen to be scratching. Damn it. I let my hand drop.

"The end justifies the means. He never peeked into our windows again."

I lift my shot glass. "To asshole men." I ignore the looks my sisters send each other and down my drink.

"Before we get this party started, we should discuss what happened," Cassie says as she mixes the margaritas.

I scowl. I don't want to discuss shit. "Didn't Sage tell you everything already?"

"She claims she couldn't hear everything."

I snort. "Seriously? She was standing in the hallway eavesdropping and we weren't exactly quiet. She totally heard everything."

Cassie shrugs. "In that case, she isn't talking."

Really? "And the miracles never cease. First, it turns out the older generation all knew about Peace's dad not being his biological dad. And now—"

Elizabeth cuts me off. "Are you serious?"

I bury my face in my hands. "Shit. I promised Peace I wouldn't tell anyone including my sisters."

He's an asshole. You don't have to keep promises to assholes, Past Olivia claims. I'm tempted. Oh man, am I tempted. I want to spill all of Peace's secrets and watch as he gets buried under them. But the anguish I saw in his eyes stays my hand. I don't want to be the cause of more hurt.

But he hurt us, Past Olivia points out. I shove her into the corner and slam the door on her. She's not the most rational person at the moment.

"Our lips are sealed." Elizabeth mimics zipping her lips and throwing away the key.

Cassie nods. "Yeah, we won't even ask the gazillion questions we have."

I glance at Gabrielle who holds her hands up. "I have no idea what you're talking about."

"What did Sage say?"

Elizabeth and Cassandra glance away, so I focus my gaze on Gabrielle.

"You and Peace had a big fight and you ran out of the courthouse crying."

I groan. "Great. The whole town knows we broke up."

Gabrielle grasps my hand. "Why did you break up?"

"He's not handling the news very well. He's lashing out. I tried to discuss it with him and he said some nasty things. Things I can't forgive him for."

She squeezes my hand. "I'm sorry."

I wave away her concern. "It's okay. I'll survive. I've been through worse."

Except no pain I've ever felt before can compete with having my heart ripped out of my chest by Peace's callous words.

"Here." Cassie slides a drink across the counter toward me. "Drink this. It'll make you feel better."

I take a sip and cough. "Or make me pass out."

She shrugs. "Either way."

"Can we watch the movie now?" I ask, desperate to prevent any further discussion of my heartbreak. Experiencing it is bad enough. I don't need to hash out the details.

"Let's go!"

Elizabeth loads the DVD into my computer while Gabrielle plates the chocolate treats she brought, and Cassie mixes up an extra pitcher of margaritas.

It sucks the man I love isn't the man I thought he was, but my sisters coming to my side to comfort me is amazing. We've never had this before. Or, at least, I haven't. Maybe moving to Winter Falls isn't the worse thing to happen to me, despite Peace.

Peace. My chest spasms but I ignore it. I'll get over him. Eventually.

Chapter 34

*Brothers – allowed to punch each other without repercussion
regardless of whether one of them is a police officer*

❦

PEACE

I open my door and scowl down at the person standing there.
"What do you want?"

Olivia's eyes flash with hurt. Fuck. I'm an asshole. I love the
woman and all I seem able to do is hurt her. It's better she stays
away from me for now. Until I get my head on straight, I'll only
end up hurting her more.

She clears her throat. "This is going to piss you off even more
but I have a surprise for you."

I hope the surprise is she isn't wearing any clothes under
her jacket. I glance down at her legs and notice she's wearing
leggings and boots. So much for a sexy surprise.

"What?"

She flinches at my gruff tone. I want to reach out and gather
her in my arms, but I burned that bridge to the ground when
I mouthed off at her and told her we're done. I am the supreme
asshole of the universe.

She moves to the side and motions to the sidewalk where Miller and Elder are standing. Elder waves our way while Miller glowers.

Anger explodes through me. "What the hell?"

Olivia holds up her hands. "I know. I know. You think you're not ready to see them."

"Think? I know my own mind. And I don't want to see them. Period. End of discussion."

She reaches for me, but I step back and her hands fall to her sides. "I lost two years with my family because I was being stubborn. Don't be me. Be a better man."

I lean forward to hiss in her face. "Don't you dare compare your hissy fit to what's happening here."

She closes her eyes but not before I glimpse the pain in them. I know I'm being a jerk, but I can't stop myself. She just sprung my worst nightmare on me. How does she expect me to respond? With smiles and kisses? Not likely.

She inhales a deep breath, and when her eyes open, the pain is nowhere to be found. "I don't want you to end up the way I did. Suffering alone without your family."

"I will never be you."

She sniffs and tears form in her eyes but she blinks them away and straightens her back. I wish I could admire how strong she's being now, but all I can see is betrayal. It's a neon sign flashing above her head. *Betrayal. Betrayal. Betrayal.*

"How could you do this to me? How could you bring them here when you know I don't want to see them? How could you ignore what I want?"

"Because I love you and I know what you need."

I rear back. "You love me?"

A tear escapes and she dashes it away with the back of her hand. "I love you."

How dare she use love as an excuse to betray me this way?

"If you loved me, you wouldn't have ambushed me."

"Wrong. It's because I love you. I would do anything to make you happy. I would sacrifice myself for your happiness."

I don't believe her. I refuse to. The woman I thought I loved would not do this to me. She would stand by my side and support me however I deem to respond to the situation.

"You should leave."

Tears burst from her eyes. "Please give them a chance," she pleads before rushing away.

Once Olivia is gone, I focus my attention on Miller and Elder. My half-brothers. They walk toward my porch and I debate going inside and slamming the door in their faces. But I'm not a coward.

I cross my arms over my chest and stare down at them. "What do you want?"

"To get to know you," Elder answers.

"Maybe I don't want to get to know you."

He huffs. "This entire situation isn't our fault."

Miller nods in agreement. "You can't choose your family."

I snort. If I could, I wouldn't have chosen this particular situation.

Elder ignores my derision. "Despite how we started—"

"We're not going to discuss what an asshole he was when we first arrived in town?"

Elder ignores Miller's question and pushes on. "Let's begin again." He reaches out his hand. "Hi! I'm Elder Bragg. It's nice to meet you."

I glare down at his hand.

Miller sighs. "I told you we shouldn't have told him."

Elder drops his hand. "He's only lashing out because he just found out. He'll calm down."

"I don't know. He doesn't appear as if he's going to calm down any time soon."

Because I'm not feeling calm. "Hey, assholes! I'm standing right here. I can hear every word you say."

Elder cocks a brow. "You can? Because you haven't listened to a damn word we've said."

I run a hand through my hair. Why the hell did I ever want brothers if this is how they act? I sense movement and from the corner of my eye, I spot Petal standing behind a tree with binoculars trained on us. Shit. I have to invite them into my house.

"Come in," I order.

"Why are you here?" I ask once we're gathered in the living room. No one's sitting. No one's comfortable. We're all on edge.

"Is he hard of hearing? Did he not hear you say you want to get to know him?" Miller asks.

"Do the two of you always have conversations with each other in front of people?" I ask.

Elder shrugs. "We're twins. You get used to it."

"I've never been around twins before."

Elder smiles. "You're in for a treat. There's another set of twins in our family."

I gulp. "Our family?"

"There are five of us."

"Two sets of twins and one lone brother who we drove nuts," Miller adds.

"Five? I have five half-brothers?"

I collapse in a chair.

"I'll get us a drink." Miller marches toward my kitchen as if he's spent time here instead of it being his first visit to my house. He returns with three bottles of beer and hands them out.

I gulp down half of my beer in one go. Fuck it. I have a ton of questions to which I need answers. They're here now. Asking them questions doesn't mean we're friends or that I accept them as family.

"How long have you known about me?"

"We found out before we moved here a few years ago," Elder answers.

"What about the rest of your family? Do they know?"

Elder glances away.

"What?"

"Our brothers don't care. They weren't interested in meeting you," Miller answers.

The souring of my stomach surprises me. I didn't expect to feel hurt because brothers I've never met before don't want to meet me.

"To be fair, our father had just died and they were grieving," Elder adds.

Our father? Does he mean my father, too? He's dead? Crap. I just found out about him and now I'm never going to meet him?

You have a dad, a voice reminds me. True. But apparently, I have a spare dad, too. What a mind fuck.

I clear my throat. "I'm sorry for your loss."

"Dad was sick for a while," Elder says. "It wasn't a shock, but still…"

Miller picks up the story. "He admitted he cheated on Mom when they were engaged while he was sick and we got to thinking and…" He shrugs.

"Considering Mom said Dad could sneeze and she'd get pregnant, we thought maybe we had more family out there somewhere," Elder finishes off.

Fuuuuck. I've been whining and complaining about my situation but I never took theirs into consideration. Their dad is gone, but mine is very much still alive and he isn't a cheater. Maybe I need to dial down the asshole.

"We had the genealogical test done before Dad died because we thought he might want to know. He confirmed the name of the woman he cheated on Mom with was Clementine."

Any hope I was holding onto about this entire fuck up being some sick joke dies a fiery death upon hearing Mom's name. There aren't a ton of Clementines running around.

"Why didn't you tell me any of this when we first met?"

Miller snorts. "Because you were an asshole."

I cringe. I hadn't realized how biased I was against outsiders until Olivia. Olivia. Shit. She was right. I did need to talk this out with my brothers.

"But you stuck it out."

Elder grins. "You're not the only one who's stubborn."

"But why stay in Winter Falls? You could have come here, met me, and gone back to your lives."

They glance at each other and I have the feeling they're doing some weird twin communication thing.

"We were at a crossroads. Our dad had just died."

"We inherited a bunch of money."

"We'd always wanted to start a brewery."

"And we appreciated how Winter Falls treats the environment."

"It was a challenge to figure out how to make a profitable business and still follow all of the rules."

"And we do love a challenge," they finish together.

My head spins from trying to keep up with how they finish each other's sentences. It's going to take some time for me to get used to it.

"Any more questions?" Elder asks.

"About a million."

He chuckles. "We're happy to answer all of your questions."

"Or we can help you figure out how to get Olivia back," Miller answers.

My chin drops to my chest, and I squeeze the back of my neck. "I fucked everything up."

"Did you cheat on her?"

"Did you hit her?"

"Did you degrade her?"

"What the fuck? No. No. And no."

I glance up and they're wearing matching grins.

"Good." Elder nods. "Then, we can still salvage things."

"I said things to her she won't forgive me for."

Miller rubs his hands together. "We got this. Hit us with your best idea."

Best idea? I have no ideas. Olivia isn't about to forgive me for what I said. I was a complete and utter dickhead. And bringing up her dead parents? I crossed a line there that I'm not sure I can recover from.

"She deserves better than me."

Elder claps me on the back. "You just proved you're worthy of her. Let's do this."

My forehead wrinkles as I study the twins. "You're serious? You'd help me?"

"It's what brothers do," Elder says.

"But I was an asshole to you."

Miller snorts. "That's also what brothers do."

"And then you forgive and forget."

"Usually after a few punches." Miller shrugs. "I'm willing to forego the punches for now. Since you didn't grow up with brothers."

Elder taps his cheek as he studies me. "I don't know. I bet he can handle a punch."

I frown at him. "You know I'm a police officer."

He bursts into laughter. "You really don't get this brother stuff, do you?" He claps me on the back again. "It's okay. We'll teach you."

I don't know if them teaching me is a good idea. Not when they're discussing punching each other.

"Are you two going to shoot the shit all day or are we going to figure out a plan to win the girl back? She is 'the one', isn't she?"

I nod at Miller. "She's the one."

He claps. "Let's get started."

Chapter 35

Boners – may be seen but should not be discussed in yoga class

❧

THE LAST PLACE I want to be today is teaching a yoga class at *Earth Bliss*. I'd much rather be lying on my sofa eating the chocolate left over from Gabrielle's last visit while sipping on cocktails Cassandra whipped up. Although, she'd need to whip up more. A pitcher of margaritas doesn't last long in a home with a heartbroken woman.

But life must go on. Or, at least, that's what everyone keeps telling me. *It'll get better. Hang in there. Tomorrow is a brand new day.* Ugh! Platitudes are not worth the breath used to utter them.

As I walk through the yoga studio toward the front door, I switch on the lights while scanning the area to ensure everything is in its proper place before the class begins. When I reach the front door, I notice a crowd of people gathered. At least I didn't escape my blanket haven for nothing.

I unlock the door and Forest barrels in. I wag my finger at him.

"You have to keep your pants on during class."

"I always do. I hate to pop a boner when I'm pantless and not around the ladies." He waggles his eyebrows.

I rub my forehead. "Pop a boner?"

"Yoga always revs my engine if you get my meaning."

Ruby pats my arm. "There. There. An erection is a perfectly natural physical reaction."

I'm aware. I'm also aware men sometimes get erections while doing yoga. It was actually discussed in one of my classes. What I'm not comfortable with is everyone standing around discussing boners.

Moon pushes her way past Forest and Ruby with a grunt.

"Are you okay?" I ask.

Ashlyn throws an arm around her best friend. "She's mooning over a man, too. Get it. Moon is mooning over a man."

Moon elbows her before marching off.

"You love me and you know it," Ashlyn shouts after her.

"Who's the guy?" I ask happy for the gossip to be about someone other than me for a change.

She shrugs. "No idea. She's not talking. Don't worry. I'll get the story out of her." She winks before following her friend into the studio.

The rest of the West sisters wave as they come inside. Behind them are my sisters and the gossip gals. Once everyone's inside, I go to shut the door but a man pushes on it before I get the chance.

"Can I help you?" The old man isn't exactly dressed for yoga.

"Don't give up on love," he states before doing a one-eighty and walking back out again.

I stare after him. "What just happened? Am I seeing things?"

Can tequila give you hallucinations? I've never had hallucinations from drinking too much before. Visions from dipping into drugs I should have stayed away from? That's an entirely different story.

"You've had your first visit from Old Man Mercury," Aspen says.

"Old Man Mercury?" I thought I'd met everyone in town by now, but the name doesn't sound familiar.

"He's the founder of Winter Falls."

"Ahem." Sage clears her voice loudly. "One of the founders," she corrects.

Aspen rolls her eyes. "One of the founders of Winter Falls. He's mostly a hermit."

"I've met him several times," Cassie says.

Elizabeth snorts. "Because your man is a fellow hermit."

"Cedar is not a hermit. He prefers the company of himself is all."

Elizabeth nods. "Which is the definition of a hermit."

"Technically, hermit is…," Lilac begins and her sisters groan. "What? What did I do wrong?" she asks but everyone ignores her.

The bell over the door chimes and I glance over in time to watch Clementine stroll inside. Great. Just when I thought I'd reached the bottom of the heartbreak well, the mother of the man I love shows up to gloat. Awesome.

"Ahem. Can I speak to you?"

I narrow my eyes on Peace's mother. She's wringing her hands in front of her while she studies the floor. Huh. This is *not* the proper gloating pose.

I wave her into my office. "How can I help you?"

"I need to apologize."

My eyes widen. This is not what I was expecting.

"I treated you badly. I'm sorry. I promise I'm working on my prejudice against outsiders."

"Okay."

"Okay?"

I'm not going to drag her over the coals. She apologized. She admitted she made a mistake. She claims she's going to work on it. She ticked all the necessary boxes for a proper apology.

I offer her my hand. "We're good."

When we walk out of the office, my sisters are waiting for me. I ignore them as I escort Clementine out of the studio.

This time I lock the door. No more weird interruptions today.

I clap my hands. "Everyone find their places."

While everyone rolls out their mats, Gabrielle sidles up to me. "How are you doing?"

And here I thought I wouldn't have to discuss feelings and other emotional crap this morning. Wrong. I rub a hand down my face.

I open my mouth to tell her class is about to begin but instead, I confess, "I declared my love to Peace and he threw it in my face."

Cassie pops up behind Gabrielle. Was she hiding? "Duh. You forced him to confront his problems. I'd probably deck you."

"You could try," I growl.

She protects her face with her hands. "Don't break the nose."

Feather shoves her way in between us. "Why would she break your nose? Is this some kink I don't know about?"

"Ew. Cassie's my sister."

"Never mind her. She's hating this month's book choice because there's not enough kink in it." Petal herds Feather away.

"Doesn't she choose the book?"

"Enough about the book," Sage declares.

"We literally spoke two sentences about the book," I quibble.

She ignores me. "I want to know what happened between Peace and his brothers."

She's not the only one. "Why don't you ask Petal? She's the one who was lurking outside of his house with a pair of binoculars."

She gasps. "She did not." She rushes off after Petal. "You told me you didn't see anything."

"Olivia," Cayenne calls from her spot in the front row where she's sitting on her mat in the perfect lotus position. "Isn't it about time to start the class?"

I check the clock on the wall. Shit. We're five minutes off schedule.

"Let's get started," I say in a loud voice and everyone quiets down as they find their spots.

Cayenne winks at me. "You'll learn to either open the door fifteen minutes early to get the chit-chat done before class or plan on staying afterwards."

In other words, this morning wasn't unusual.

I lead the class through my centering routine before beginning the warmup. As the exercises in the warmup never change, I can switch off my mind and concentrate on how my body feels until it's time for the core sequence.

When the warmup is finished, I begin the core sequence of inversions, forward bends, backbends, twists, and standing poses. Since I didn't spend any time preparing for today's class

– add the inability to care about your job to the column of why heartbreak sucks – I run through a standard routine I know by heart.

"Our next exercise is a standing split."

I walk amongst the group and correct posture. When I reach Aspen, she announces, "I'm ready for a handstand."

"But we're not doing handstands."

"I've been practicing at home."

"Against a wall. A freestanding handstand is completely different," Ellery points out.

"I bet she can't do it," Ashlyn taunts.

"I'll take your bet," Juniper says and they slap hands.

"No. No. No. No betting. A handstand isn't a move you can suddenly perform. You need to prepare your body properly."

"I got this," Aspen declares as she inverts into a standing split. Only this time she doesn't stop with one leg in the air, she throws the other one up, too.

Her arms wobble and I reach out for her but she falls over before I can get there. On her way down, she takes out Ellery and Lilac.

"And down they go," Cassie shouts

"I can't believe it wasn't me," Elizabeth murmurs.

"You're admitting you're a klutz?" Cassie asks and Elizabeth growls at her. "Still living in the land of denial."

I separate Aspen, Ellery, and Lilac. "Is anyone injured?"

"If you say yes, River will show up in his firefighter uniform," Elizabeth chimes in.

"I think my elbow hurts," Clove hollers.

I roll my eyes. "You weren't involved in the accident."

She waggles her eyebrows. "Have you seen River in his uniform?"

"Is everyone in this town sex-crazed?" I ask the room.

"I wouldn't use the word crazed," Forest answers.

"There's nothing wrong with sex," Ruby says. "Why just the other day Daniel and I—"

Ashlyn groans. "No, Mom. We discussed this. You agreed to not discuss your sex life with Dad in front of me."

Her mom gasps. "I would never agree to such a thing."

"I want to hear the story about Ruby and Daniel. Who's with me?" Sage asks and every member of the gossip gal gang raises their hand. Normally, I'd join them, but I don't have any inclination to listen to how awesome other people's sex lives are when I'll probably never have sex again.

"Is class done?" Ashlyn asks.

"We still need to cool down and relax."

She sits on her mat and crosses her arms across her chest with a scowl on her face.

"Now you know how it feels when people continue to babble on and on about things you don't want to talk about," Moon teases.

Ashlyn wags her finger at her friend. "Don't you dare compare my parents having sex to you withholding information from me. They are two completely different situations."

"Relaxation time," I announce and everyone finally quiets down.

We do a series of cooling floor postures before moving into Savasana, aka corpse pose. I indicate they should hold the pose for at least five minutes without moving or thinking.

This is usually my favorite part of a yoga class. When I've completed the hard work and can relax and let my mind float. Except my mind insists on being in the here and now today. The here and now where my heart is broken and the man I love hates my guts. Shit, I need to—

A snore cuts off my thoughts. It's not uncommon for students to fall asleep during Savasana. Usually, they don't snore, though. Forest snores again. I guess I should be happy he decided to snore instead of pop a boner today.

Gabrielle giggles, which sets off Ashlyn and pretty soon everyone's laughing as they stand to gather their things and leave. Cayenne kicks Forest to wake him and he joins the exodus.

"Come on." Cassie links her arm with mine. "Let's go have pancakes at the diner."

"I don't want pancakes."

"Gracious has pancakes loaded with chocolate chips," Gabrielle says.

"Oh, in that case."

I allow Cassie to drag me across the street to the diner where I eat pancakes the size of my head and try to forget all about the look of betrayal in Peace's eyes when I surprised him with a visit from his brothers.

Chapter 36

Fruitcake – completely loveable whether soaked in alcohol or not

❧

PEACE

I pace back and forth in the yoga studio as I wait for Olivia to show.

"You're going to wear a groove in the brand-new floors we just laid," Miller says.

I run a hand through my hair. "What if she doesn't come?"

Elder grasps my shoulders to stop my non-stop pacing. "Her sisters promised to get her here."

"Her sisters are none too pleased with me at the moment."

I can't blame them. I threw Olivia's declaration of love back in her face. Does this mean she no longer loves me? I sway as my legs nearly buckle at the idea.

"Olivia's sister Cassandra is a babe. Is she available?" Miller asks.

I growl at him. "Cassandra is taken, and you will not hit on any of Olivia's sisters. You got it?"

He chuckles. "Just checking."

"Checking?" What the hell is he talking about?

Elder rolls his eyes. "He's wondering if you have the big brother gene since you didn't grow up with siblings."

"There's not a big brother gene."

"You obviously didn't have siblings growing up. There's definitely a big brother gene. Just ask Damon who is no longer the big brother. You are."

Wait. What? This is news to me. "I'm the oldest of six brothers?" And the hits keep on coming.

"Shush," Miller calls from near the entrance. "I think they're nearly here."

I guess I'll process the big brother thing later. No time now.

"You two hide in the office." I shove them toward the small room.

"Oh. Are we your dirty little secret?" Elder waggles his eyebrows.

"Seriously? You've lived in Winter Falls for years now. You know there aren't any secrets here."

"Except no one knew we were brothers," Miller points out.

I shut the door on him. This is a discussion for another time. I'm thinking never.

Footsteps approach and I switch off the lights before rushing to crouch behind the reception desk.

"You have got to be kidding me," Olivia complains. "How is the place flooded?"

"Because there's water everywhere on the floor," Cassie answers.

"Don't be a smartass. You know what I mean. Is the toilet broken? Did someone leave a faucet running? I can't believe this. I don't have the money for new floors and new plumbing."

"You have the money," Elizabeth chimes in. "You can use your trust fund."

"Yeah," Gabrielle adds. "Beckett said you can have access to it again since they caught the guy who stole your money."

Geez. Are they going to stand outside the studio discussing this all day? My knees are killing me after spending two days laying the floor in this place.

"Whatever," Olivia mumbles as she unlocks the door and switches on the lights.

I jump out from behind the desk and throw my arms in the air. "Surprise!"

Her eyes narrow on me. It's a good thing she can't shoot lasers from those things or I'd be stone cold dead.

She snarls at me. "What are you doing here?"

I lower my arms. "Surprising you?"

She crosses her arms over her chest and taps her foot. "And why would you surprise me? You want nothing to do with me, remember? I betrayed you and lied about loving you."

What did I think? She'd see the new floors, new equipment, and new furniture and rush into my arms? Yeah, I guess I kind of did.

"I'm sorry. I shouldn't have…"

My words trail off when I notice her sisters creep closer so they won't miss a word. Is there anyone who lives in Winter Falls who isn't a gossip?

I march to her. "We should discuss this in private."

"Discuss what in private?"

"Do you want me to spill my guts in front of your sisters?"

The door bangs open. "And brother," Beckett announces.

"And sister-in-law," Lilac adds.

Cassie raises her hand. "I vote for spilling his guts in front of everyone."

"I agree," Beckett grumbles. "Then, I'll know how badly I need to beat him up."

I ignore them and keep my attention focused on Olivia. She studies me for several long moments before sighing. "Privacy would be good."

I don't give her a chance to change her mind. I grasp her elbow and lead her to her office. The door opens before we arrive and my brothers spill out.

"What are they doing here?"

"They helped."

She smiles at them. "Thank you."

I growl. Them she smiles at? I'm the one who paid for everything. Who drove to White Bridge three times to pick up supplies. "What about my thanks?"

She snorts. "Dream on."

I herd her into the office and slam the door behind us.

"I need to—"

Her gasp cuts me off. "Whose furniture is this?" She doesn't wait for me to answer. "Wow. This desk is gorgeous." She runs her hand over the surface. I want her to run her hands over me in the same amazed way. Soon. I promise myself. Soon.

She plops down in the office chair and props her feet on the table. "This chair is super comfy."

"Are you done admiring the furniture?"

She takes her time scanning the room before nodding. "Yes, I believe I am."

I move to stand beside her. She drops her legs and scooches the chair away from me. My heart sinks. I deserve her drawing away from me, but it still hurts to witness how she doesn't want to be near me.

I drop to my knees in front of her and her eyes widen as she scrambles backward until the chair hits the wall and she jolts to a stop.

"I was an asshole," I say and her eyes return to pissed off woman.

"You won't hear me arguing with you."

"I didn't deal with learning I had another family very well."

"Ya think? Go on."

"I should have handled things differently. Instead of pushing you away, I should have leaned on you. The woman I love."

"W-w-what?"

I grasp her hands. When she doesn't pull away, I take it as a sign things are going my way.

"I love you, Livie. I've loved you since the day we painted this studio and you showed me how much fun hard work could be. No, wait. I started falling for you at Lilac's wedding."

"Ha! I got you beat. I started falling for you when you showed up at my new apartment with a coffee mug to welcome me to town."

My heart hammers in my chest. "You still love me? After the things I said? I should have never brought up your parents and family the way I did."

"True." She nods. "But apparently love is not a water tap you can switch on and off at your own discretion. Why do you think I wanted you to patch things up with your brothers even after we broke up?"

I shrug and she releases my hands to squish my cheeks together. "Because I love you, you silly, silly man."

And I thought my heart was hammering before. Now, it's trying to beat a path out of my chest and straight into Olivia's hands.

"And you forgive me?"

"I'm not sure. I don't know if there's been sufficient groveling."

"In addition to the furniture in here, I put in new floors and bought you some new yoga equipment."

She shakes her head. "I'm not talking about buying things, although what you've done in here is marvelous and I can't wait to see the rest. I'm talking about realizing the mistakes you made, accepting the consequences, and being willing to do better in the future."

"I learned my lesson. I lived without you for over a week. I don't want to ever wake up without you next to me in bed again. I will never behave the way I did this past week again. I will never lash out at you in anger again. Let alone bring up stuff from the past just to hurt you. From now on, I will always treat you the way you deserve."

"Which is?"

"As my queen."

She smiles. "You're a quick learner."

I can't resist those luscious pink lips any longer. I mold my mouth to hers and she groans before grasping my shoulders and pulling me near. I thrust my tongue into heaven and moan. God, I missed the taste of her mouth. The feel of her beneath me. My hands wander to her breasts.

"Um, guys?" Cassie yells before knocking on the door. "I hope you're dressed because there are some people out here you might want to meet."

I draw away from Livie's mouth. "Who?"

"You have to see it to believe it."

I clasp Olivia's hand. "You ready for whatever surprise is waiting out there for us?"

"Or we could lock the door and I could have my wicked way with you?" She waggles her eyebrows. The little temptress.

"Not to ruin your naked party or anything but I can hear everything you're saying," Cassie hollers.

Olivia frowns. "Raincheck?"

I smack her lips in a quick, hard kiss. "Definitely. You ready?"

She squeezes my hand. "Ready."

When I open the door, Cassie indicates the three men gathered near the entrance with Miller and Elder. Based on their resemblance to each other, I know who they are.

"It's my other brothers."

"Your other brothers?" Olivia asks.

"There are five in total."

"You really know how to throw a surprise party," she mumbles.

Oh shit. This is her day. "I can meet them some other time."

"Why? They're literally half a room away. Why wait?"

"This party is for you."

"I admit I'm selfish, but I'm not that bad."

"You're not selfish. You're wonderful."

"Gag." Cassie feigns throwing up. "I've got the gossip. I'm out of here if you two are going to be all lovey-dovey."

Olivia ignores her sister and squeezes my hand. "You ready to meet them?"

"With you at my side, I'm ready for anything."

"No worries then. Because I'll always be by your side."

Before we can go meet my brothers, Moon screams, "What the hell are you doing here?" Before slapping one of the men across the face.

Olivia barks out a laugh. "I think I like your brothers already."

"Fruitcake."

"Fruitcake you love."

I kiss her nose. "Fruitcake I plan to love and adore for the rest of my life."

Chapter 37

Fake it 'til you make it

🦋

MOON

I glare at the door as if it's the reason I'm in a foul mood. To be clear, it's not. The door hasn't done a damn thing to me. Except exist, which at the moment, is enough to anger me.

To be fair, just about everything makes me mad at the moment. Because my life is officially falling apart. Boom! The pieces of the perfect life I was building scatter to the winds never to be found again. I promise I'm not being dramatic.

Don't believe me? Here ya go:

My kitchen faucet exploded in my face today.

My contractor up and quit on me.

All my friends are in love and utterly disgusting.

And, here's the kicker, my boyfriend ghosted me.

Although, a weekend with a guy does not a boyfriend make. Stupid me. I thought we connected beyond the fabulous sex. We stayed up all night talking in bed. Didn't that mean something to him? Obviously not.

"Whatcha doing?" Ashlyn asks and I scream.

I whirl around to confront her. "What are you doing sneaking up on me?"

Her eyes widen and she points to herself. "Me? Sneak up on anyone? Have you met me?"

"Yes, I met you in kindergarten when you were digging for boogers in your nose and I showed you the error of your ways."

She narrows her eyes on me. "I was not digging for boogers."

I snap my fingers. "Oh yeah. I forgot. You stuffed a Lego piece up your nose."

"It was for experimental purposes."

I cock my brow. "Such as? Finding out how painful it is when the school nurse digs a Lego piece out of your nose with tweezers?"

She shivers. "It was freaking painful. I never stuffed anything up there again."

"You're welcome."

"Are you done procrastinating now?"

"I'm not procrastinating."

She snorts. "You're glaring at the door to *Earth Bliss*. What did it do to you? Steal your underwear?"

I shrug. "I don't feel like going to a party is all."

She gasps before laying her hand on my forehead. I bat her away.

"Are you sick? Do you have a fever? Do you need me to phone Dr. Blue?"

I frown. "I'm not sick."

"You're not heartsick?"

This is what I get for having a best friend who doesn't hesitate to use your secrets against you.

"Why are we friends again?"

She smiles and laces her arm through mine. "Because I'm awesome. You're awesome. And together no one can stop us."

After her announcement, I can hardly stop her when she barges into the yoga studio where there's a party for Olivia today. Her boyfriend, Peace, majorly screwed up and did this big grand gesture as an apology. And, because this is Winter Falls, the event became a party.

I don't need a stupid grand gesture. I just want someone to show up. Even when times are tough. Or boring. Or whatever times were when Riley ghosted me. It's not as if I have a clue what happened. And if there's something I hate more than not knowing, I haven't figured it out yet.

"There's my big teddy bear," Ashlyn coos before skipping toward her husband.

Rowan is not a teddy bear, but he is as big as a bear. As in six-feet-five-inches-tall and built like a linebacker. Except he wasn't a linebacker, he was a quarterback. And he has the Super Bowl ring to prove it. My best friend doesn't give a dam about his fame, though. She's loved him since she was old enough to understand boys don't have cooties.

Ashlyn leaps at him and he catches her before spinning her around. He's shaking his head at her, but the smile on his face clearly says he'd do anything for his dream girl.

I want that. I more than want that. I thought I had that. I was wrong. I was deceived. I was cheated. I was lied to. I was—

You have got to be kidding me. I rub my eyes with my fists to clear my vision. It can't be. Nope. He's still standing there. I blink my eyes to clear them. Shit. Still there. Just when I thought my life was done going to hell, I discover there's another circle of torment. Awesome.

I stomp toward the big fat liar pants. "What the hell are you doing here?"

And, then, before my brain can catch up with what I'm doing, I slap *him* across the face.

"Moon?"

"Yeah, Moon. Are there any other women waiting in the wings to slap your lying face?"

"This ought to be good," a man mutters and I focus on him. He's a carbon copy of Riley.

"You must be Brody."

He grins. "I'm the handsome twin."

"Are you an asshole, too? Does it run in the family? Or is the assholeness limited to this one?" I thumb my finger toward Riley.

"Hey, now." Elder steps in front of Brody to protect him. Protect him?

"What does this have to do with you?" I snark at my boss. Maybe not the best idea, but he won't be my boss forever. Although, considering the whole life falling apart thing, he may be. Crap. I'm going to end up being the hostess at *Naked Falls Brewing* for the rest of my life.

Now is not the time to consider how my life has turned to shit. Nope. It's the time to settle scores.

Riley shoves Elder out of the way to stand in front of me. "Can we talk?"

"Now, you want to talk? Un-freaking-believable."

"Will you let me explain?"

"Explain!" The word explodes out of me. "As if an explanation could ever be good enough for what you did."

He flinches. "I'm sorry."

"Save it. Why don't you and your brothers return to whatever hole you crawled out of?"

Peace clears his throat. "Ah, Moon. These are my brothers."

Crap. This is what I get for not paying attention to the rumors for the past month. Blindsided. I scan the faces in front of me and realize it's true. The resemblance between Peace and the five other men is undeniable.

I'm still not apologizing to Peace. He may be a police officer, but he's not on duty now. Which means he's just your average citizen and I can shove my boot up his ass without repercussion. Metaphorically, of course. I can't literally shove my boot up anyone's ass. I don't even wear boots.

Olivia slaps Peace's arm. "What are you doing? You never stop a woman in the middle of a smackdown. It's against all the rules." She nods to me. "Go ahead, Moon. Make him rue the day he met you."

I don't want Riley to rue the day he met me. I want him to rue the day he ghosted me. I want him to yearn for me at night the way I yearn for him when I'm lying in my cold bed wishing he was in it with me.

I smack myself upside the head. Stop this nonsense. I don't yearn for him. I refuse to want someone who can so carelessly toss me aside. I'm worth more.

I glance up at Riley and my body warms as tingles spread throughout my limbs. Why does he have to be this handsome? Why can't I forget how it feels to have him touch me? To have him make love to me?

I clear my throat. "Whatever. I'm done."

I whirl away and stomp to the exit.

"Moon," Riley calls and my hand freezes on the door. "I'm not letting you go again."

I glance over my shoulder. "You didn't let me go the first time."

With those parting words, I shove my way through the door and hurry outside. I don't need to look back to know the entire town of Winter Falls have their noses pressed to the windows of *Earth Bliss*. I've lived here my entire life. I know how nosy everyone is. I'm usually one of the nosiest.

I lift my chin in the air and stroll down Main Street as if my heart isn't breaking. I can fake it. And I will. Until I make it.

Chapter 38

Let me make a call

🦋

"I need to grab some fresh clothes and then I'll be over," I tell Peace over the phone. "Love you."

Yep. That's me. Telling a man I love him like it's nothing. Except it's not nothing. It's freaking everything. Peace is everything. The grand gesture, which I refer to as the 'groveling on his knees apology', was several months ago and we're still going strong.

My life is actually fantastic. I never thought I'd get here after waking up in my bedroom in Saint Louis and realizing a man I barely knew had stolen all of my money. But here am I and I'm here to stay.

Peace is building a relationship with his brothers and *Earth Bliss* is doing well. I started a weekend yoga retreat together with Lilac's sister, Ellery, who runs the local bed and breakfast and it's booked up months in advance.

I finished one of the yoga retreat weekends today and I am exhausted. My body aches from two days of exercise and my head is killing me from handling rich entitled people for the entire weekend. It pays the bills, I remind myself.

I open the door to my apartment to discover it empty. Completely and totally empty. What the hell? Everything I own is gone. How did this happen?

I drop my bag and rush to the kitchen and open the cupboards. Empty. Someone cleared out my entire apartment. I fish my phone out of my pocket. I need to notify the police.

My phone is snatched from my hands and I scream. "Get away! I'll break your nose."

"Oh no. Not my nose," Peace mocks.

"Thank goodness you're here. I need to file a police report."

"A police report about what?"

I throw my arms out to the sides. "I was robbed!"

"You weren't robbed."

"I don't care what the technical term for it is. Someone stole all my things. Who's on duty? Call Freedom. Call Lyric. Yes. Definitely call Lyric. The Chief of Police should be here for a crime this big."

He chuckles before handing me a rose bush.

"Why are you giving me a rush bush?"

"Because Eden doesn't sell cut roses."

"You're making no sense. This is an emergency and you're acting like nothing's wrong. Something is definitely wrong. All my stuff is gone."

I sniff as I feel tears well in my eyes. I can't do it. I can't begin again from nothing. I just can't. What will Beckett say? And Cassie? The 'I told you so's' will never end.

"Livie," Peace murmurs before drawing me into his arms. "Don't cry. This is a happy occasion."

I burrow into his hold. "Happy occasion? Are you crazy?"

He kisses the top of my head. "I think I might be. Because I thought it was a good idea to surprise you this way."

I wrench myself away from him. "Surprise me? Is this your doing? What were you thinking?"

"I was thinking it'd be fun for you to come home and discover your home is now with me."

"Fun? Home is now with you? You're making zero sense. I need to sit down." I scan the area. "But there are no chairs!"

He raises his hands in surrender. "We've been discussing moving in together for a while now, yes?"

"Yes."

"And we decided my house was the place we want to live, yes?"

"Yes."

"But you didn't want to move because you've been too busy with these yoga retreats."

"Don't you dare give me a hard time for working too much. I'm building a business."

"I'm not. I'm not. I'm proud of you. Haven't I told you as much?"

I consider it. Has he said he's proud of me? "No, I don't believe you have."

"I'm an idiot."

"No argument from here."

He grasps my hands. "Olivia Lucy Dempsey, I am proud of you. You amaze me every day with your work ethic, your determination to be a better person, and your out of the box thinking to make your business a success. All of it humbles me."

My eyes sting and now I want to cry for a different reason. "No one's said they're proud of me since my parents died."

"Fuck, Livie," he murmurs before wrapping his arms around me and holding on tight as the tears spill from my eyes.

"I miss them. My dad would love you."

He rocks me back and forth. "He would?"

"His troublemaker settled down with cop? The dad jokes would be endless."

"You're not a troublemaker."

I giggle. "The troublemaker hasn't left me. Trust me." *Past Olivia* waves and mouths *I'm still standing.*

He wipes the tears from my cheeks. "Livie, do you want to move in with me?"

I nod. "Yeah."

"You want to sleep in my arms every night?"

"Definitely."

"You want to wake up next to me every morning?"

"You know it."

"Will you forgive me for moving you into my house without telling you first?"

"As long as there isn't some big party waiting at your place."

"Our place," he insists.

Oh, I like the sound of that. "I want to celebrate this occasion with just the two of us."

"Shit. Let me make a call."

My eyes widen and he bursts out laughing. "I'm kidding. I'm kidding. You're not the only one who wants to celebrate with just the two of us." He waggles his eyebrows.

I grab his ass and knead the muscles there. "We could start a celebration here."

"Yes, please!" Sage shouts and waves from the hallway.

"Hi, Sage," Peace greets before shutting the door in her face.

"Peace Reed Sky! I changed your diapers!" Sage screeches from the other side of the door.

"Now, where were we?"

"You were about to ravish me." I wink. "Assuming you can catch me."

I sprint down the hallway toward the bedroom. He catches me at the entrance to the room and throws me over his shoulder before smacking my ass.

"I think someone needs to be punished."

Oh, goodie. Now, this is how you celebrate moving in with the man you love.

"I love you, Peace."

"And I love you, troublemaker."

About the Author

D.E. Haggerty is an American who has spent the majority of her adult life abroad. She has lived in Istanbul, various places throughout Germany, and currently finds herself in The Hague. She has been a military policewoman, a lawyer, a B&B owner/operator and now a writer.

Made in the USA
Monee, IL
03 October 2024